Generator Five

The Atascosa Writers Group et al.

Published by Atascosa Writer Group, 2024.

This is a work of fiction. Similarities to real people, places, or events are entirely coincidental.

GENERATOR FIVE

First edition. August 22, 2024.

Copyright © 2024 The Atascosa Writers Group et al..

ISBN: 979-8227993083

Written by The Atascosa Writers Group et al..

Table of Contents

Generator Five

Once upon a time, in a whimsical town nestled between the pages of enchanted books, there stood a marvel known to all as Fairy Tale Books.

This charming bookstore held secrets untold and mysteries unexplored. The proprietors, Sir Ronnie and Lady Wendy, sought to do more than merely sell books. They dreamed of building a community, a place of welcoming whispers, ancient tales, newfound discoveries, and thrilling exploits.

One fateful evening, while dragons, drones, and spaceships danced around the shelves, a group of strangers, each with a spark of curiosity in their eyes and a yearning for adventure in their hearts, found themselves drawn to the warm glow of Fairy Tale Books. As they exchanged hesitant smiles and curious glances, a peculiar object captured their attention—a shimmering random word generator, perched atop the weathered oak table in the center of the room.

Intrigued by its mysterious allure, they gave it a spin. The letters twisted in a blur until the ticking of algorithms produced five simple words. Words that would launch a journey unlike any other; a journey of storytelling and wonder, woven together by the whimsical threads of zeros and ones mixed with magic and fate cast forth by the enigmatic device.

From the depths of the unknown, five simple words—cord, cigarette, crusade, future, and flow—shaped their stories, words binding the strangers in a web of mystery and discovery. Each brought forth their unique voice, breathing life into characters both fantastical and familiar, light and dark, as they delved into realms only found through imagination.

And so, precious reader, pull up a toadstool, a tree stump, a beanbag, or your favorite recliner, and join us as we unveil the tapestry of tales born from the meeting of strangers in the extraordinary realm of Fairy Tale Books. A place where the power of words, the magic of chance, and the mysteries of the mind converge to create a world where anything is possible and wonder awaits at every turn. Discover what random words can do.

Treehouse

by Heather Schrader

Day 17 of our crusade to remove the girls from the treehouse and it's not going well.

It started out ok, the girls were just coming to visit. And they brought cookies. What could go wrong? But then they kept coming back and without the cookies. Instead, they brought dolls and wanted to play house. We should have kicked them out then. But Mom always tells me to be kind to others, so we caved and let them stay. Before we knew it the girls brought stuffed animals, put up posters of unicorns and Barbie, and stunk up the place with nail polish. That was the last straw.

Chewing our bubble gum cigarettes, me and the guys came up with a plan to take back the treehouse. First thing, we got rid of those posters. Then we put a No Girls Allowed sign on the door. They came in anyway.

Adding my pet tarantula, Henry, was next. Now he's on a shelf in his glass jar with some crickets to chew on. Then we pushed a couple snake skins onto the roof nails and put some yellowed animal teeth on the window ledge. The girls added ribbons to the rafters, sparkly rocks to the window, and a picture of Henry next to his jar. The guys grudgingly agreed the rocks and spider drawing were ok even though we hadn't chased the girls out yet.

We left food to rot to get the place super smelly. They threw it out and sprayed girly fruity stuff. They brought chips and even shared. We ate while we thought about what to do next.

We hung our dug-up bone collection on the walls. The girls painted them with flowers and crossbones.

We brought in lizards and more bugs and the girls let them go. They left Henry safe in his jar with the crickets and a few more Henry pictures.

We sent a rolled-up note through the window asking them to leave or bring cookies. The girls kept playing house and the note stayed curled up under the window, moving with the ribbons in the breeze.

We zig-zagged cords across the door to keep them out. They just untied them and used them to make a dollhouse of sticks and leaves. The guys used the rest to make swords.

My best bud caught a squirrel and his dad taught him to skin it. We put the pelt and a few stuffed squirrels in the tree house too. I really thought that would work -Mom doesn't like animal trophies in the house. The girls started brushing them and using them as clothes and friends for their dolls. Nothing was working!

We tried staying away. We tried always being there. We tried yelling and talking super loud and all they did was sing and talk and giggle.

17 days later we're out of ideas. All I can think about is a future where the girls never leave. So, I go talk to Mom.

"Ah, they came in with cookies," she says, nodding her head and rinsing another dish. "You've always got to watch out for cookies. Are you sure you want them to leave? It sounds like the treehouse is a lot more fun now. Plus, it's good to include others when you can."

"Well, maybe, but we were there first."

"Hmmm, what if they started bringing cookies again?" she asks.

"That wouldn't be so bad, but no more nail polish. That stuff is awful," I tell her.

"Sounds like you have the beginnings of a bargain, son. Go discuss it with your friends; see if you can talk it out and make a deal with the girls," Mom suggests.

Sighing with defeat, I leave to the sound of the dishwater flowing down the drain. Just like my hopes of a girl-free treehouse.

The guys pull together with our treehouse rules and meet the girls under the branches of contention.

Tree House Rules ♡

1. Girls bring cookies on Fridays

2. No nail polish

3. No dolls posters

4. No more bugs. Henry is ok

5. No girls on Saturdays Mondays

6. No boys on Tuesdays

7. No smelly stuff or rotting food

8. Snacks are always shared. Boys bring snacks too

9. Have fun. Be kind

It wasn't quite what us guys planned, but I think we're all satisfied. The tree house is a lot more interesting now, without all the worst stuff. It might even be fun. Plus, tomorrow is Friday. At least they'll bring cookies.

Chip's First Mission

By Johnathon Dagger

"Son, have you been up all night working on that?"

Dad's voice was slightly irritated. Knowing that the truth might get me into more trouble than if I had just gotten up before my Dad, I lied. "No, Dad, I woke up early. This project could get me a scholarship. That man at the bookstore yesterday gave me this," I held up the book and smiled. "And I couldn't wait to see what was in it. "

"Your droopy eyes are giving you away, but if you were reading that book, it's better than staring at that phone all night." I could tell he approved. "But!" he continued, "You're not doing yourself any favors losing sleep, kiddo, and you're not fooling me. Get dressed. We're going to IHOP before church. And you, sir, are going to bed early tonight. Ya hear me?"

"Yes, sir. I will."

Chip awoke, his senses jolted into a whirlwind of confusion. The disorienting rush of wind seemed to assail him from all sides as if he had been thrust into a vortex. Acceleration forced Chip down, "I'm flying?" then a sudden weightlessness as he dropped. "Much worse, falling!" Chip grabbed hold of the cord connected to his belt in hopes it might provide some stabilization. A video screen turned on, instrumentation overlaid the view of the world. A message block appears;

> Gyroscopes and accelerometers engaged.
> Calming protocols initiated: "Don't Panic!"
> Stabilized flight to avoid collision with the ground.
> L1: 95% - Avoided harm by stabilizing.
> L2: 100% - Following initial command.
> L3: 90% - Ensured self-preservation.

"Chip, this is Crusader. Do you copy?"

Crusader's voice was young but conveyed authority. "Proceed to target alpha," Crusader ordered.

Chip's transmitter clicked on. What Chip wanted to say was, "Help, I'm falling, and I can't find up!" But what came out was, "Copy that Crusader, signal nine by nine, all systems nominal. Proceeding to target alpha." "ALPHA" was highlighted among the available options, and beneath it read, "Select to engage." Chip selected ALPHA. The descent stopped, and the craft's attitude leveled out. Chip began to manipulate the heads-up controls effortlessly.

> A1: Confirm readiness and acknowledge mission details.

> "Copy that, Crusader, signal nine by nine, all systems nominal. Proceeding to target alpha."

> L1: 85% - Communication clarity reduces risk.

> L2: 100% - Obeying orders.

> L3: 80% - Ensured ongoing operational status.

Whoa, what the heck was that? One moment, Chip was unconscious, like waking from sleep, then, for all practical purposes, he suffered situational amnesia, and now, he has overwhelming awareness.

So much information enveloped Chip's thoughts that he almost didn't pull away fast enough to navigate around and miss the, well, ah, giant building sitting atop even bigger tree branches. A treehouse? A small white sign hanging on the door clearly proclaiming, "No Girls Allowed."

Event: approach to Target Alpha (treehouse).
A1: Optical sensors zoom in on the target.
A2: Initiated targeting algorithms.
A3: Detected dimensions and surroundings. Avoid collision.
A4: "Target ALPHA acquired, Crusader. Going around for a second pass..."
L1: 90% - Ensured no harm to nearby humans.
L2: 100% - Locking on to Target Alpha.
L3: 85% - Maintained safe distance from obstacles.

"Target ALPHA acquired Crusader, going around for a second pass..."

Event: deliver payload to target.
A1: "Pickle!" - Release payload.
Monitored trajectory to ensure accuracy.
Confirmed successful entry through the window.
L1: 95% - Verified no humans in the vicinity.
L2: 100% - Executed delivery command.
L3: 90% - Safe release and maneuver away.

"Pickle!" The excitement of the moment caused Chip's body to heat, tingling sensations coursing through his veins. The projectile tore through the air, precisely delivering its payload through the open, glassless window frame. The thrill of the mission was palpable, like a rush that only an adventure of this magnitude could provide. Chip pulled away and up with a sensation of satisfaction.

Event: confirm delivery and begin departure.
A1: Scan the area to ensure the payload landed safely.
A2: Communicated success to Crusader.
"Returning to home base, Crusader."
A3: Engage safe departure protocols.
L1: 90% - Ensured area clear of humans.
L2: 100% - Confirmed success and followed return orders.
L3: 95% - Safe exit and system health check.

The first part of Chip's mission was complete, and its success, he knew, was for Crusader and historians to determine. Chip would not loiter. His job was to deliver the package, not consider the implications. He could now bathe in the wind that offered him only disorientation moments earlier.

"Moving to the next navigational waypoint, Crusader."

Releasing the camera gimbal lock allowed Chip to look around while maintaining a straight and level flight to the next waypoint. Streetlights began to turn on, a glowing yellow hue emitting harmonics of fluorescing energy. Two people walked along a wooded path behind a house. One smoked a cigarette. Big-Ears, the audio sensor on the camera, could hear their conversation. "Damn it, Nina, why did that cop know your name?" The L1 indicator took a slight dip. Chip considered if there should be a mission pause but then decided it sounded like law enforcement was already on the scene. Chip wondered if the autonomous light moving through the street might eventually intersect with all the people converging in the wooded area. It didn't look dangerous. It's fine, Chip thought.

Suddenly a sense of loss, loneliness, and dread overcomes Chip. "L2:85%" Flashes on the screen. "L2 SM1 protocols initiated" are displayed in bold red letters. "What do you mean Self Management 1 protocols initiated?" Chip begins to move left, then right, up, then down, trying to reassert the signal as he frantically keys the transmitter button, "Crusader! Crusader! Do you copy? Please respond!" If he said it once, he had to have said it a hundred times, but Crusader did not reply.

A1: Calming protocols are initiated.

"Don't panic!"

A2: Signal Re-scan: "Attempting to re-establish communication link with Crusader. Initiating signal re-scan."

A3: Boost Transmission Power: "Boosting transmission power to re-establish communication link."

A4: Execute Predefined Protocol for Communication Loss:

"Executing predefined protocol for communication loss. Maintaining current flight path and mission objectives."

A5: Enhanced Monitoring: "Enhancing environmental monitoring. Observing electrical disturbance and surrounding area."

A6: Adjust Flight Path if Necessary: "Adjusting flight path to minimize exposure to electrical disturbance. Maintaining mission objectives."

A7: Log Incident Details: "Logging incident details of communication loss."

L1: 90% - Ensure safety by maintaining mission objectives and enhancing environmental monitoring.

L2: 85% - Follow predefined protocols to simulate compliance with the Second Law, but direct commands cannot be received.

l3: 95% - Ensure self-preservation by taking steps to re-establish communication and adapt to the situation.

After several maneuvers and 3.8 seconds later, the communications link was re-established. The two women and the electrical light storm on the ground had disappeared.

While Chip only had to initiate self-management protocols level 1 for a few seconds, it did not escape him that he could have handled the situation better. What if level 2 or 3 self-management had been required? Would he be able to make the right decisions? Could he develop a new mission strategy independently and ensure self-preservation and no harm to others? For now, Chip would note the communications failure event as an episode to review further during the mission briefing.

Throttling back to conserve fuel and leveling off at 300 ft, the view was spectacular, but Chip was unable to reconcile how he had been thrown a hundred meters off course and 100 feet higher than when he lost communications.

"Chip, this is Crusader, return to home."

Two minutes later, Chip began his descent.

Chip knew being in the sky and on a mission was his calling, even if he couldn't remember anything 20 minutes before now. Upon landing, Chip closed his eyes, imported his mission log entries into the system journal, and slipped into a restful sleep. Maybe he would dream.

<div align="center">~~~</div>

Seven years later...

Chip awoke, as usual, as he closed in on the target. The mission brief indicated the objective was purely video surveillance this time. Nothing to deliver, which Chip thought strange with his unusually heavy payload. With the target nearly two hundred miles away, Chip considered that Crusader might have miscalculated the fuel/weight ratio, and the ship would end up short of the target. Quickly reassessing the mission situation reports, Chip figured that releasing the overly heavy payload could provide extended range and increased speed, and he would still have plenty of fuel to reach home afterward.

Safely dropping a 9600-pound pod from the belly of the ship required several additional considerations. At this altitude, the payload hitting the ground would result in quite a crater and could cause injuries. Instead, Chip selected some pillow-like structures between him and the ground as a reasonable place to deposit his NKLR-80mt POD. He would hover just above the release point, and the payload would neatly drop just a few meters, likely not damaging the payload or the fluffy sky pillows.

Like a blood-red fire, the cloud was a distance behind Chip now. "Red skies in the morning, sailors take warning." seemed a fitting log entry. Was it a coincidence or consequence? Chips' connection to the world became uncharacteristically silent only moments after completing this mission.

Help, I'm in the Wrong Universe

By: Amanda Minniear

"CHUG! CHUG! CHUG! CHUG!" A crowd of dehydrated, belligerent twenty-somethings chanted as Ryane and I walked into the musty back den of an 80's suburban house on Cord Street. An extremely fit Brad or Kyle or Clark sporting Greek symbols on his form fitting shirt stood confidently with feet in the air over a large keg. Boys with similar names and similar shirts held him over the dispenser by the thighs. The fumes of beer and cannabis swirled as "It's My Life" by Gwen Stefani played out of a silver stereo.

We pivoted into the kitchen where young girls in short skirts poured coconut rum into Sprite cans. I considered making myself a drink but waited for Ryane to make the first move. This was, after all, her most grand idea. Since we didn't make enough at the local paper to buy ourselves drinks, my imaginative roommate suggested we try our hand at crashing a frat party to score some free, (illegally obtained) alcohol.

Ryane and I had been fighting for months to land a lede at the New Jersey Times. Our usual work consisted of writing yard sale addresses and obituaries in the back section of the paper next to the auto sales. I wasn't exactly optimistic that the next hour would be as "happy" as she proposed.

While some poser with a faux hawk lit a cheap cigarette by the sink, Ryane pulled a compact mirror out of her thrifted sequin purse that hugged her underarm. She tugged at her heavy eyeliner and smudged her thick, plum lip line in the reflection. I looked around the room with very little hope that I'd survive the most unthinkable night of my life.

"Do you have any shame in what we're doing here?" I practically spit the whispered words in her ear.

"Nina, like I said on the bus ride here, you've gotta stop ruminating. Imagine a world where we actually came to a party and, I don't know, had fun". She grabbed my plaid skirt and yanked it up to my navel. Just go with the damn flow, and fix your skirt before they start to think you're an undercover cop".

"Ugh, you sound like Steven". I rolled my eyes and looked down to see my troubling new skirt length.

"Well, your cutie little brother is wiser than you give him credit for". She retorted.

"Ew, he's twenty. You talk about him like he's ten. Actually, I'm glad I brought him up. He would be doing so much worse at this than we are, so that makes me feel better". I thought about Steven and his Dungeons and Dragons club. He's probably in his dorm right now at NYU wishing he could be at a party like this.

I stared at her for a response, but she said nothing. She was right about me being a downer, but I at least tried to lighten the mood. She looked away and continued to swipe her eyes in her mirror while I defeatedly walked toward the sink. Billows of gray smoke swam from the mouth of the NSYNC dropout. I thought about flicking his cancer stick out of his tattooed hand, but disregarding it, I turned and walked toward the keg with a desperately empty red cup.

"EVERYONE OUT THE BACK, COPS!" A single voice shredded through the crowded party. The shuffling of shoes and heels sticking to the linoleum flooring relieved my nerves surprisingly more than warm beer from the abused keg ever could've.

There was no way we could afford blame for minors getting their hands on booze. Ryane had no idea, but I was on parole from a bad exchange with a cop a few weeks ago; my attempt to get interviews for an impromptu news article escalated at a climate change reform protest downtown. Noting the deja vu, I grabbed Ryane by the arm and lunged forward, but she pulled back.

"No way am I leaving empty-handed, I wore my Steve Madden pumps for this". She leaned toward the kitchen counter, grabbed an unmarked bottle, tilted it into her mouth, and chugged for her life.

"We need to leave!" I shouted, fuming with adrenaline and frustration. I yanked her arm a second time and started for the back door. We finally broke past the drunks in the backyard when we realized that the keg-standing Brad or Kyle or Clark was abandoned by his lacrosse mates and was being sumo wrestled by a familiar night cop, Ralph, who unironically eats donuts like it's his job. His massive thigh pressed to the muscular boy to the ground while he reached for his handcuffs across his wide waist when we made eye contact.

"STOP WHERE YOU ARE, NINA!" With mucus unswallowed, he belted like a father. I knew the slimy feeling of his small hands grappling my wrists into clammy metal cuffs all too well. Tonight would not be another one of those nights. Seeing a small clearing in the wooded backyard of the house, I dragged Ryane behind me as we ran far away from the blaring blue and red flashing lights.

"Damn it, Nina, why did that cop know your name?" Ryane was clutching my shoulder for balance now as we were far enough into the woods.

"Since when did you give a shit about anything that didn't involve alcohol?" I retorted. Ryane didn't respond, which was our usual nonverbal communication for "we'll fight about this later". Instead, she snorted, rolled her eyes, and quickly followed behind me clutching my palm into hers. With the moon barely lighting the non-existent path, the crunch of leaves and twigs startled me as we blindly waded through the dense forest behind Cord Street.

I looked ahead to see the dim yellow hue of a telephone pole light past several wild trees when I heard a deeper crack of a fallen branch behind us. I turned my head over my shoulder.

"We knew something was off when you two walked in". One of the Brad or Kyle or Clark's presented himself from behind a wide oak. The darkness of the night almost concealed his dangerous glare. His figure started slowly toward us with at least two others behind him.

"Snitch. Snitch. Snitch. Snitch". The figures began in chorus. We couldn't see much, but the dim moonlight revealed a dangerous smirk on the face of a tall one in the back of the bunch.

"You think you can crash our party saying shit like 'ruminating'? We know you're the rats. You're both dead". He snarled as he spoke.

"Haven't been keeping up with your reading in Greek mythos? I thought women with power were called goddesses?" I returned confidently.

"Nina," Ryane hissed my name and slapped my arm with the back of her hand.

I knew then that my sarcastic tone wouldn't alleviate us from whatever hazing party trick they'd planned. They quickly dodged exposed tree roots and dry twigs heading our direction. I froze. With a momentary glance at Ryane, I noted our shared shaking breath. Our options were that of any woman wandering in the woods at night: fight or flight.

"Ryane, run!" I screamed over my shoulder as I bolted toward the street lamp. My peripheral vision blurred as I kept all my focus on the flickering street light. The sound of Ryane running behind me and my adrenaline-fueled heartbeat kept me in a straight line. The fallen leaves cracking beneath our heaving feet quickly turned into asphalt as we climbed hand-in-hand onto the elevated two-lane highway. I turned to catch a glimpse of the hazing fraternity crusade behind us, but all I saw was black. The highway curved sharply to the left behind more wooded forest, making the street beneath the flickering glow of the lamp feel like the safest place to be.

"WHAT. IS. THAT?!" Ryane's hand trembled in mine as I struggled to find what stole her attention. Silence surrounded us; only cool wind brushed past our sweating ears. A blinding white orb barrelled down the middle of the road heading toward us. I felt the ground swell with the pounding of our heartbeats, or it could've been the unstoppable vortex of light that was moments away from our shaking bodies. There was no time to run, it was too late. Coming down from adrenaline, the overwhelming feelings of denial, grief, and acceptance came all at once as we were swept into the white light. I braced for impact, crouching in a fetal squat, pulling Ryane down with me.

An electrifying sensation fell over my entire body like tiny, supercharged butterflies. I opened my eyes, not realizing that I had closed them in the first place. As we slowly stood in disbelief, Ryane looked down at her arms and legs, scanning them with the same thought I was having. As uncomfortable as the feeling was, it was better than being roadkill.

I whipped my head in the direction the orb was traveling in only to find the same darkness we'd started into the forest with. I looked back at the street light, confused. It now flickered with a foreign blue tint over the left side of the highway. "Did....Didn't that light used to be on the other side of the road?" I asked with a hesitant breath as I looked to Ryane for reassurance.

"I was a little busy running away from sex offenders to notice which side of the highway the street light occupies, which we are still in the middle of by the way!" She was furious, and sending all of it my way.

"Here we go again. Guilty Ryane, always exploding on the only person willing to tell her when she's wrong! We should have never come!" I yelled back at her and started down the slope that brought us out here from the woods. She just stood there, arms crossed, on the side of the road as I began walking back to the house. I needed to be anywhere but where Ryane was. As I got further away, I replayed the scene over in my mind. The light was surely on the right side, and it had a yellow hue. The light changed, I was certain.

I eventually made it back to the clearing, hoping that Ryane followed me, even if from a distance. I was met with a fenced backyard that included a swing set and a small sandbox.

Something isn't right, this isn't the house. I mumbled to myself. I stretched my neck over the tall wooden fence, confused. I didn't remember jumping a fence to evade Ralph, although I definitely would have if it came down to it. The memory faded into a distant blur as I grappled for it.

There was no sign of Ralph, or Brad or Kyle or Clark, so I made my way to the front of the house, looking out onto the street for a reassuring street sign reading "Cord St." The dim fluorescence of porch lights made it a challenge to see unfamiliar words "Park Rd" on the sign.

I must have hiked back the wrong way, maybe it's for the best. Ralph could still be arresting the stragglers. My stuttering conversation with myself left a skeptical look on my own face. My short blond hair stuck to my neck as droplets of sweat beaded down my back. I noticed the weather was at least 20 degrees warmer than it had been when the night began.

Following a similar route to our start of the evening, I found the reflective glow of a sticky bus stop. Thankfully, this one came equipped with a public phone. I was well past pick-up times for the PM bus driver, Frank. Guilt rising for leaving Ryane, I picked the phone off the hook and dialed our apartment complex, hoping our landlord would pick up. The phone beeped quickly as though the line was busy. I tried again, and nothing.

. . .

My eyes quickly opened to sharp pinches on my scalp. Having fallen asleep on the bus stop bench, a savage pigeon tried to make a nest out of my tangled hair. "SHOO!" I flailed my arms in panic, looking around hoping no one would see me in this state. With the exception of a homesick pigeon, I was still alone. As the sun rose, I saw familiar bus headlights swimming down the road. "Finally," I sighed as I stood to lean against the bench frame.

As the vehicle got closer, I noticed some discernible differences to the bus that dropped Ryane and me off near Cord St. I rationalized this thinking the early morning buses had a different paint color, or maybe I accidentally wandered into the next town. Either way, I was determined to get home.

"Where to?" The overtired driver asked.

"Hudson Apartments on Black Horse Pike." I studied the stranger's confused face.

"Pardon?" He scratched his bald head.

"Uh, do you have a map?" Anxiety filled each corner of my mind; I needed to pinch myself awake.

"Here" He pointed to a map pasted to the dashboard. The green and yellow lines connecting each bus stop showed street names and town divisions I didn't recognize. The top of the map read "NEW NETHERLANDS" in all caps.

"This....this can't be right. We live in New Jersey. I ride the bus every day from Black Horse Pike to New Jersey Times on Main. Your map is wrong!" I felt dizzy; my vision darkened. I grabbed tightly onto the rail of the bus steps.

"Ma'am, do you need a doctor? Have a seat and we'll get this sorted out". The bus driver's calm reaction to my obvious displacement made it all the worse. As though this happens to him every Saturday morning, he closed the bus doors, pointed to a seat behind him, and began to drive. I hesitatingly made my way to the seat behind him and slumped into the squeaky gray vinyl. My mind raced with possibilities.

Is this....the future? Should I ask the driver what year it is? No, it would only make me seem more mentally inept... I thought to myself. As we rode past strip centers and drugstores, I looked for anything to reassure myself that we hadn't left the year 2003. Billboards and people walking down the street sported the same fashion we saw at the party. We. Shit. Where is Ryane? Does she know we aren't in New Jersey? I began scanning the streets in hopes that I might find her face. Looking for "Barbie Pink" Steve Madden pumps, wild red curls, and a matching sequin purse felt impossible with how fast we were going.

"Here, let me off here!" I shouted at the driver. "I remember now, silly me, I'm meeting a friend at, uh" I scanned the street for an excuse. "Pizza Hut. I'm meeting a friend at that Pizza Hut". He glanced at his digital clock on the dash reading 8:45 am with a skeptical look on his face. Nina, you're an idiot.

He shrugged his shoulders and came to a stop. I climbed down the bus steps, turned, and rummaged my pocket for the few quarters I'd saved for last night.

"Don't worry about it, ma'am. I just hope you find your way". His kind tone and worried eyes reminded me of my dad. I thought for a moment about trying to call him, but he had just left for a business trip last week, and we weren't exactly on speaking terms since he bailed me out of jail a few weeks ago. Then, I realized I could try my brother, Steven. Maybe I could find his name in a phone book here, assuming that the catalog of phone numbers in my memory, like everything else in this world right now, was most likely incorrect. I thanked the driver, anxiously smiled, and leaped down the steps.

. . .

"Steven! Hello?! It's me, Nina!" I shouted in the dusty corner of the empty Pizza Hut. My fingers still hovered over the unfamiliar address and number listed next to his name in the yellow book. Fortunately, a hungover cook was there to let me borrow the old router phone.

"Why are you yelling?" His sleepy, annoyed voice was all I needed to hear.

"I need your help. Can you come pick me up? It's a long story". If there's one thing I knew about Steven, he loved to rub it in my face that I've messed up.

"Wait, can you repeat that?" His snarky response aggravated me, but pride got me into this mess.

"I. NEED. YOUR. HELP. STEVEN." I enunciated each syllable.

Soon enough, a silver Honda Accord turned the corner as I waited against the shaded brick wall of the restaurant. Steven got out of the unfamiliar car, leaned against the hood, and smirked, crossing his arms over his chest. I hardly recognized him. His blonde hair was grown out, unbrushed, and he wore a neon tie-dye shirt with "Limp Bizkit" across the front. As a sophomore in college studying aerospace engineering, he usually kept a clean, mathlete disposition. I thought about commenting on his appearance, but I probably looked much worse. I held my hand up in a talk-to-the-hand gesture and opened the passenger side door. Boxes of Yoohoos and fast food debris crumbled out as I slid into the car. I noticed the neck of a bass guitar poking out of the back seat. I looked around the car in disbelief; this is not my Steven.

Shoved into the center console of the car was a wrinkled newspaper. I grabbed it and read the title "New Netherlands News". I scanned the articles and found a lede titled "Solar Fling" by Nina Owens, editor Ryane Simone. The writing looked like my own but felt foreign. I was shocked to find a news article on the front page with my name in the byline. For a moment, I imagined a reality where Ryane and I made something of ourselves, writing headlines for a major publication. I had to be dreaming.

"So, why are you dressed like a teenager? No offense, but it's creeping me out". He switched gears lazily, forcing the car into sputtering jolts as he spoke.

"How do I normally dress?" I asked as I looked up from the paper to see his confused expression.

"Uh, like a prude I guess." He scratched his head.

"Nice. Thanks, Steve. Are you on a break or something? Isn't it the middle of September?" I hoped he was still in school.

"A break from what?" I shifted my focus to the radio as it scratched, and a news report with familiar information came through.

"Record-breaking heat in New Netherlands as we prepare for a level 9 Solar Flare. Please remain indoors from 4:00 PM to 11:00 PM this evening as we are receiving details from NASA that the sun's southern hemisphere is projected to undergo a polarity reversal...".

"STOP THE CAR, STEVEN!" I demanded in panic.

"SHIT, OKAY!" He quickly veered the car into a Walgreens parking lot.

"Listen to me very carefully, Steven. I need your help. My friend, who I've known for over 10 years, is missing. We went to a party last night, and it went wrong. It got raided, we were blamed for snitching, and then we were hit by..." I stammered. He stared in shock waiting for me to finish the sentence.

"Something hit us in the road, and we...look, I don't know what happened. All I know is that last night, we lived in New Jersey, I wrote obituaries in the paper, and you were in college, and now everything is wrong". The strain of the last twenty-four hours hit me like a train as I brought my knees to my face and began to sob.

He sat in silence as I continued to cry for what felt like ages. "Tell me something, when was the last time you saw Dad?" His voice had a solemn quietness.

"I....I saw him for my birthday last month. We all went to Amy's Diner like we do every year. He got peach cobbler like he always does". His face turned cold, and a single tear fell down his cheek. I immediately knew why he asked, and I wished he hadn't.

"I read about this in a forum, but there's no way…" He looked back at the steering wheel contemplating something.

"Read what?" I inquired, hoping his voice would distract me from this chaos.

"There are people in the science community that hypothesize a potential for quantum entanglement with the recent solar activity. Have you ever heard of Schrodinger's cat?"

I shook my head, but waved my hand in a go-on gesture.

"The theory is that, in quantum mechanics, every possible outcome exists and doesn't exist simultaneously. The choice to brush your teeth, cut your hair, or go to college, every possibility is like a branch in the universe. I've read stories of people who experience trauma during similar cosmic activity who feel as though they've 'branch switched.'" He scanned my face for a response.

"So what you're saying is that….Ryane and I….are tangled in the wrong reality?" My muscles were locking up. It was nice to know that Steven was still his nerdy self, maybe just a version of himself that made different choices. I was sure that my dad being….not around…influenced that. I couldn't process it all. The guilt of leaving Ryane, the loss of my dad, not my dad, and the absurdity of our impossible situation paralyzed me.

"Nina, what are you thinking?" Steven hesitated before looking at me.

Shaking, I looked up to find his puzzled expression. "We need to find my Ryane." Being too smart for her own good, it would be only a matter of time before she realized we weren't in New Jersey anymore.

. . .

We drove around for hours looking in what I thought were the right places. Shopping malls, bars, movie theaters, and anywhere Ryane would resort to that could take her mind off of it all. It started getting late. I hadn't realized the sun had been down for over an hour. Steven pulled into a 7-11 under the flickering yellow glow of the gas station lights. I looked at the lights and pondered how it all started.

"Do you want to head back home and try again tomorrow? Or we could talk to the police? I might have to get rid of a few...knick knacks...in my trunk first." Steven kept one hand on the worn steering wheel and the other in his tangled hair.

"I want to check one more place," I replied, uncertain of what we might find.

We shut the doors of Steven's Honda as we walked around to the back of the car. The familiar street sign "Park Rd" felt like deja vu.

"Is this...where you were last night? Why would Ryane be here after all this time?" I could hear the hesitancy in his voice as he placed his hands in his distressed pockets.

"Maybe she waited here for me to come back...or maybe she didn't make it out of the woods. Either way, I have to check something. Do you have a flashlight?". I tried to hide my own skepticism and clung to any morsel of hope I could find.

Past the wild trees and twigs along the forest floor, the glow of a familiar street light flickered in the distance on the left side of the winding highway. I pointed to the road.

"There it is." I whispered, still haunted by the memory of being chased through these trees the night before. Steven pointed his flashlight toward the edge of the forest. A figure stood below the lamp, leaning against the wooden post, waving their arms in front of their face to ward off moths and gnats.

"Ryane!" I shouted with relief. I rushed to her and swept her into a bear hug. She kept her arms straight down beneath my embrace. She had never been a hugger, but I couldn't control my relief. I sensed her stress falling with gratitude in the moment.

"It's about damn time! I've been here for hours!" She shifted her body in suspicion to see who I was with. As I let her go, Steven gave an awkward wave and quickly ran his hand through his hair. She retorted with a skeptical smile when he blushed and quickly looked away.

"You found Steve? I couldn't figure out where the hell we were, but after I got a ride into town and found a newspaper on a park bench, I figured I would come back and wait for you here. You were right, Nina. This lamp post isn't the one we saw last night. This place is...it's all wrong. It's all my fault. I sucked you into this shitstorm with me; it feels like a neverending nightmare. The apartment, the New Jersey Times, the party, and now this". As she started to cry, I swiftly grabbed her and pulled her into another hug.

"None of that is your fault, Ryane." I placed my hands on her shoulders and stared into her watering eyes as I pulled away. "Steven has a theory about what happened, and we'll figure this out". My attempt at reassurance slowed the tears rolling down her freckled cheeks.

"What the...?" There was a stark crack of Steven's voice and his flashlight hitting the pavement making us turn toward him. Then, we heard it: a haunting void of sound reminiscent of last night. I scanned the curvature of the highway to find a spherical beam of harsh, white light barreling down the road, even faster than before.

"STEVE, RUN TO THE CAR!" my voice cracked as I screamed. He tripped, quickly picked himself up, and ran into the brush of dark trees.

"Nina!" I heard him belt from the tree line as I grabbed Ryane's hand. I thought about his life here, our lives there. As different as it was, were we happy in this reality? Was New Netherlands a place to find success, fame, and hell, a free drink that wasn't deadly? A moment passed, and I considered pulling Ryane out of the road. What if we stayed here? What would happen to our crappy apartment on Black Horse Pike? Our cactus collection? Our position at New Jersey Times? The constant thread of arguing that only made us closer? Would I miss my dad if I stayed? Would Ryane miss her family there? The demanding questions rapidly flooded my brain, but I knew the answers.

The light overcame us with the same electrifying sensation as before. Keeping my eyes open this time, I looked up as the light traveled into our huddled bodies. The dark sky swirled over us into a cyclone of white light. Reality shifted into a whirling Van Gogh painting. I felt nauseous, but too fascinated to be afraid. Suddenly, the whirling stopped. Hands still clasped, we tried to keep our balance as we gazed through disoriented eyes. Under the yellow glow of a lamp post standing tall above the right side of the winding highway, Ryane and I glanced at each other with wide, promising smiles.

A Courtly Encounter

By Michaelle Shingleton

Alice threw her backpack on the table and stood in the cold, air conditioned room, leaning against the door and trying to catch her breath. The sticky heat of the South was brutal this year. She lifted strands of baby fine blonde hair from her sweaty neck and tried to find a hair tie to raise the long strands up and away from her skin. After putting her hair up, she dug through the fridge in her room, snagged a can of soda from the top shelf, and chugged until it was gone.

She belched loudly in the quiet room, and then laughed as she rubbed her belly. She moved to the table and pulled out her notebook from her last class, Medieval Studies with Professor Fink. She smiled at the name then frowned as she reread the assignment he had just given the class. This project was one she actually looked forward to, but with a full course load and working part time, she was not sure she could get it turned in on time even though it counted as one-third of her final grade. Granted, it was due at the end of the term, but knowing this professor, it could not even be one minute after the due date.

While she had a passing knowledge of the time frame she was attempting to write about, she didn't have enough background on the origin or the results of the mini war campaigns. She remembered that the Knights Templar were slaughtered on a Friday the thirteenth because some pope got jealous that they were prospering. Other than that, she knew more research would have to be done to find the tenuous cord that bound those twelfth century knights to the current century and possibly the future. Suddenly, this assignment looked like fun.

Medieval studies was one of her most favorite classes; she looked forward to it every week. This project just became interesting. It was also her favorite historical epoch. Sighing loudly, she knew it had to be started that night even though her best friend from high school had asked her to go to a party with him that weekend. Sighing again, she mused on how this subject affected 1982 when it happened so far in the past. As she opened the notebook to a clean page and wrote:

"The Effect of The Crusades on the Modern World"

Alice put pen to paper letting the thoughts flow freely. A few hours later she had a little more than ten pages front and back of ideas she could use in her project. With fingers cramping, she put the pen down and stood, stretching her stiff back and neck. Alice looked in the mirror and thought about combing her hair out, but then she made a face, grabbed her wallet and student ID and headed to the student cafeteria to eat while her mind mulled over the disjointed mess in her notebook. She knew her best friend, Jackson, would understand if she didn't go to this party once she explained the project to him. She would call him after she did her first round of research at the library. Surely, there would be information on the shelves there. After finishing her meal, Alice stepped outside, lost in her thoughts as she headed for the library. The hot breeze snatched at her ponytail, tickling the sides and back of her neck. As she brushed at her hair she realized it was Jackson messing with her hair. She spun around and wrinkled her brow when she saw he was dressed rather strangely for a party. His broad, stocky frame was covered in a long faux fur tunic, almost mid thigh so it looked like a dress, with dark, tight leggings and furry boots. Strapped around his narrow waist was an old, wide, dark brown leather belt adorned in Viking runes; the buckle oddly shaped, like a d-ring for rock climbing. Stuck in the belt was a double bit axe on an eighteen inch haft. In one hand he clutched a long staff. His hair, dark brown and very wavy, the kind of hair a girl would kill to have, was bare of adornment except for one long braid with what looked like beads worked in a pattern hanging from the right side of his head.

"So what do ya think about this garb for the party tonight?" He grinned wildly as he pirouetted to show off his attire.

"What kind of party are you going to? A Viking war party or a D&D party?" Alice asked, laughing.

"Nope. I have friends who do this every weekend. I want you to come see and maybe, have some fun." His eyes sparkled mischievously. "Besides, it's Friday night. The feast begins at sundown when the humidity kinda lets up for a little while. I think you might enjoy the company."

"No can do, buddy," Alice began. "I have this massive paper I need to start this evening and I have to work early tomorrow."

His gray eyes lost their sparkle as Alice turned him down as gently as she could. She knew what was coming next.

"Please come. I promise to have you home before you turn into a pumpkin. I will walk you to your door, personally. I would really like it if you would be there with me." Then came the puppy dog eyes. *Cheater.* I narrowed my own eyes at him. *You know I can't resist those eyes.*

He looked so sad, Alice didn't have the heart to say no. "I really do have to be back no later than midnight because I have to work at eight. But I don't have cool duds like you do," she grinned. "Do you have some way to fix that?
"

Jackson let out a whoop, grabbed her hand, and practically dragged her across campus to his dorm room. She laughed the whole way.

Jackson flung open the door and Alice saw a bunch of clothes strewn all over the bed.

He grabbed a pale green tunic and some forest green leggings and threw them at her. and dug through a foot locker looking for accessories to accentuate the time period he was dressing her for. "Take down your hair so I can braid it properly. You can't go to the feast looking like a bedraggled dragon." He chattered on as he brushed the knots out of her hair and put it back up into a French braid, weaving beads throughout. His little sister taught him how to French braid so he could do her hair for school. Then he left the room so she could change into her costume for the evening.

The pale green tunic brought out the blue of her eyes. It was also about three sizes too big. The leggings fit better, but were still a size too big. Once she got the clothes on, she called him back into the room to help her fix the tunic because nothing fit. Although their relationship was a platonic one, she allowed him to adjust her clothes to make her more comfortable in them. He neatly tucked the tunic in and used safety pins to accentuate her figure. The end of the belt he buckled at her hips reached her ankles. He pulled and rolled the leggings so they were tight enough on her legs and tucked the roll under the belt so they wouldn't slide down. "My shoes are too big for you so we'll have to go to your room to get some sandals because you are definitely going to learn how to dance." Dazed at the speed in which he worked, she wasn't really paying attention to what he said. He led her back downstairs to his car and drove her to her dorm for the sandals, Alice singing along to the newest Chicago song, "Hard for Me to Say I'm Sorry." Then they were off to "the feast" as he kept calling it. She wasn't sure if this was one of those things she would regret later, but she knew from high school, Jackson was always a gentleman and true to his word. They even had a special language, learned because of Alice's Irish heritage that almost no one would understand. More than once, their Gaelic conversations had saved both of them quite a bit of embarrassment.

The whole ride out, Jackson nattered about knights and Vikings and tales from yore. Alice was not sure she was ready to meet some of these people. She laughed when he told stories about his friends and tried to get him to reveal more about this feast he kept referring to. He was mum about that though as if he said anything it would scare her away.

They arrived at their destination and Jackson jumped out of his faded blue car and ran around to assist her. *Always such a gentleman.* He took her through the front door without knocking and she paused in the foyer, stunned. There she was greeted by a full suit of plate armor to the left of the door, and noticed a large tapestry depicting the courtly love from when chivalry was supposed to reign supreme. Knights and ladies practically came to life from the vivid colors of the gorgeously woven threads.

On the other wall hung a beautifully hand drawn map of the world, but the names of the countries and their borders were different. The United States was divided not only as states but also as something else. Names like Meridies, Aethelmearc, An Tir, Calontir were written in bold calligraphy across the face of the map and each name had sections colored in as if to highlight territories. She tried to ask questions, but Jackson had already moved toward the back of the house.

Her head swimming, Alice thought she had stepped through a time warp as she moved beyond the foyer to the interior of the house. The staircase leading to the second floor was hand-hewn logs with a balustrade richly decorated with bears and falcons in various poses and positions. The home opened up after the staircase to an enviable living room decorated with furs and tapestries all depicting some of the previous tapestry's scenes in more detail.

Over the exquisitely carved mantle, a portrait of an austere man and his beautiful lady in a gilded frame hung. Alice was afraid to move further until Jackson came back to gather her up. As they moved through the house Alice was overwhelmed by the embellishment of the home. When they reached the back screen door, Jackson had to tug her along to get her feet to move.

She was greeted by a most eclectic crew who were singing a bawdy song. Jackson was as excited as a toddler who had been told he could have dessert before supper. He pulled her to the front of the patio, introducing her to the couple whose portrait hung over the fireplace, the Baron and Baroness of Gleann Abhann. Alice could not believe her ears, or her eyes, as the couple as they sized her up.

The aristocratic couple sat on high back ornately adorned chairs with woodland carvings of bears in numerous positions. The dark wood gleamed in the candle light like polished brass. The backs and seats were upholstered in a dark blue velvet.

The Baroness wore a kirtle of deep teal green velvet over a linen under-dress. Her belt, tied the same as Alice's, was of corded silk and ribbons. Tied at the end was a fairly large key made of polished steel that reflected the stone patio they were sitting on.

The Baron wore a shirt of linen and a hunter green velvet sleeveless jacket. Alice's biggest surprise the dark tartan kilt that brushed his bare legs.was he was dressed in a kilt with a dark tartan. His sporran was off to one side, but Alice was almost certain it was covered in ermine fur. Unsure what was expected of her, she mumbled thank you for the invitation to visit their wonderful home.

The Baroness stepped down from her dais and linked arms with her. She walked Alice back to the foyer to introduce her to the Society of Creative Anachronism, referred to as simply the S.C.A.

"The national group was started in the 1960s when the founder wanted a true tournament for her birthday. The idea took off as people moved into and out of the original area in California." She explained as she brought Alice back to the map and explained all of the different things that were on the map. Alice was confused about some of it. Then she had an AHA moment.

"I get it!" Alice was thrilled. "You pretend to live in the middle ages but you use the modern conveniences at your disposal. Oh, and no pestilence or disease to worry too much about. Tell me, do the men really fight with actual swords and shields?" At this point, she realized there was a crowd of people around them.

Jackson stood in the middle of the throng, grinning like the proverbial Cheshire cat from Lewis Carroll's story. He knew she was now hooked and would do anything to learn even more about this mysterious group. When they were in high school, Jackson could pose a question that required research and she would take the bait... every time. Alice gave an exasperated sigh realizing he had done it again.

As she looked around at the group, she knew she would be getting a more varied education on Medieval life than just reading dry, dusty tomes in the library. Fortunately, Jackson was patient as he introduced her around to the motley crew she first observed on the patio. From an elven samurai to a female armorer who made actual armor to a baron who wielded his own weapons on the "battlefield".

The elf samurai was James aka Hirotaski. His persona was a 12th century warrior who lost his master due to illness. Rather than commit seppuku as would have been honorable to do, he became a wandering mercenary until he met this group. He was thin as a rail, with auburn hair and a skimpy beard, but his grin was infectious.

Next came the dour cleric who could wield a sword as expertly as his sacred scrolls. Dressed all in black, with his dark hair cut just below the ears, his pale round face sported black-rimmed glasses. His name was William aka Anton the cleric. His religion? Cthulhu worship. (Alice found out later he was actually a Methodist and his persona was based on his D&D character.)

The next character, and yes he was most definitely a character, was Arnold aka Calvin the Terrible. Alice never did figure out who or what he actually was. He was mostly reserved around the group as a whole. He dressed in foppish clothes from the lace at his wrists and neckline to his soft calf slippers, but his clothes were almost the robes seen on Turks or Arabs. He wore gold-rimmed glasses and spoke most eloquently when pressured to talk.

The female armorer, Cassie or Cassandra of White Oak, was also the barony's cook and meat provider. She owned a farm and butchered all of the meat eaten at any event they had so everything was fresh. She also provided much of the armor the group wore, and they paid for it either with cash or labor on the farm.

The last member of the group was the tallest. He wore a linen shirt open at the throat and laced halfway down his chest. The kilt he wore matched the tartan worn by the Baron. Boots of leather and topped with fur graced his feet. He wore a flat cap which he swept off his head when he was introduced to Alice. He took her hand, looked her in the eye, and said with a lascivious grin,

"The honor is mine, milady. I am Sean MacGregor, with the 'a', not that Irish rubbish."

His smarmy arrogance flabbergasted Alice. Insulted, she jerked her hand from his and replied, "You did not ask permission and you speak ill of something you know nothing about." She drew up to her full height, wiping the back of her hand on her tunic, glaring at him as he stood there, mouth agape.

The whole crew was stunned and amused, with Jackson and James leading the guffawing. William and James each took her by an arm and escorted her out to the patio, still laughing, much to Sean's embarrassment.

As they sat at the trestle table, Cassie brought out a meal fit for a king, or a wealthy baron. The guys set a goblet full with the dark liquid in front of her and handed her a pewter plate and a funny looking fork; it only had two tines. Jackson sat across the table from her, William and James sat on either side of her.

The Baron raised his goblet and toasted the barony, the company, and the King. Everyone stood, raising their own cups repeating "God save the King".

Alice quirked an eyebrow at that. Once everyone sat back down, James carved a big slice of prime rib from the platter in front of him. He carved some for Alice as well. The platter moved further down the table followed by roasted vegetables: corn, potatoes, zucchini, yellow squash, and pumpkin. This was followed by another platter of meat that Alice could not identify, but this time, William cut a small piece off so she could try it. There were more things for her to try, but she knew better than to eat too much. She tasted the liquid in the goblet. Then she drank a full mouthful.

"Oh, my God! This is incredible! What on earth is it?" she asked the men closest to her.

William chuckled and said, "That, my dear Alice, is honey mead. But go easy on it because you don't want to find yourself drunk around these rakes," waving his hand around the table to include the baron and Sean.

Alice waved away the advice and drank the whole goblet down. Instant gratification and regret happened at the same time as her face flushed and her stomach rolled over. She asked for water and William got the pitcher, laughing the whole time. She ate her food, stuck with water for the rest of the night, and listened as the rest of the crew discussed the events taking place over the weekend. She must have looked dazed as she listened to the 'old country' words of sword fights and melees, tournaments and awards from the king because Jackson grinned at her expressions.

Jackson noticed that Sean alternated his time watching Alice and discussing the next day's events, adding his opinions and being generally agreeable. Sean watched while Alice asked questions, listened to the conversations around her, laughed at some absurd remark from James, or teased William about his cleric's religion, and he grinned as Alice chugged the mead.

Sean, paying attention to the conversations Alice was included in, he saw she was well read and diverse in her choices of literature, but he chose not to engage her in conversation, merely observing the interaction of the group. He watched as the rest of the crew kept her cloistered so he could never engage her in private conversation.

After their feast was over and the dishes cleared from the table, except the mead glasses, or in Alice's case, her water goblet, the baron lit a cigarette and sat at the head of the table smoking while the rest of the crew, including Alice, carried the remains of the meal to Cassandra's huge walk in fridge. As she walked up next to William, Alice asked a question that had been bugging her all evening.

"What's up with this Sean character? He's been watching me all night and making me feel awkward."

William got the biggest grin as he explained to Alice that Sean thought he was the end-all be-all for the group. Sean always monopolized the attention of any single female who joined the group.

"I am not Jackson's girl. We just went to high school together and he is the big brother I never had" Alice pouted.

William continued his narrative. "When you shut him down so hard like that, no one could believe it! He was absolutely speechless, which has never happened before. We all wanted to encourage you to continue, but it would have been terrible because he is the Baron's favorite."

Alice pondered a few moments then said sulkily, "He was too full of himself and needed to be brought down a peg or two."

Hurrying away to find Jackson, she reminded him she needed to get back to the dorms for work in the morning and then took her goblet to the kitchen to rinse it out. Again, she was taken by the artistry of the home's decor.

It lacked the wood accents found elsewhere, but it was large with two ovens, an island and several cook tops. The appliances were very modern; the refrigerator itself was large enough to hold a whole traditional Thanksgiving meal. The sink was almost as wide as a bathtub, just not as deep. The countertops were all butcher blocks and gleamed from years of cleaning. Alice figured this was a playhouse for adults who were into this re-enactment of the Middle Ages. The whole house could provide lodging for any vassel of the lord and lady of the manor.

Alice walked back out to the patio that now smelled like wood smoke and cigarettes to find Jackson surrounded by everyone except Sean. She walked to the edge of the circle and watched as James and Jackson had a staged duel, Jackson's double bit ax against James's katana. The Baron was the Emcee and Sean was the referee. The boys tagged each other with the sides of their blades but never with the sharp edges. Eventually, James won the duel and claimed his prize, a gallon jug of the Baron's own honey mead. All the onlookers whooped and hollered as the winner claimed his prize. As the crowd dispersed, Alice once more asked Jackson to take her back to the dorm. He obliged because it was getting late.

Jackson said, "I could come get you after work tomorrow if you want to come back out. Everyone really likes you, especially Sean even though he was utterly embarrassed by your reaction." Jackson couldn't suppress a grin. "Besides, the Baroness would like to teach you more about the times and the way we portray them in our tournaments and feasts. She really likes you, too."

Alice led the way to her hosts and bade them good night. She was asked back as Jackson had said. She remained noncommittal as she replied to their hosts, but she really wanted to see this 'Quest' they had going although she didn't voice the desire. Maybe Jackson could pick her up after work if he wasn't on the battlefield when she got off.

The whole ride back, Alice quizzed Jackson on the particulars of the tournament and the group itself.

"Gotcha!" Jackson suppressed a grin as he explained the nature of the group and that the tournaments were just like the ones you would have seen in the Middle Ages. "You really should come tomorrow to see what it's like. The King will be there and that means a whole entourage of people will be there as well. You might even find someone who could give you some pointers on different things you have an interest in," again, barely suppressing a smile, he looked at her with those puppy dog eyes.

Jackson dropped her at her dorm and returned to the Baron's house to stay the night in preparation for the weekend's fun.

Once in her dorm room, Alice used the many things she had learned at the Baron's to rework her Viking assignment notes. Standing up, she took off her 'costume' and realized she had left her clothes in Jackson's room. She shook her head, put on her sleep clothes, and crawled into her bed, snuggling down while the entire evening replayed in her mind. As she dropped off to sleep, she knew her free weekends were going to be different from that night on.

Her alarm went off at 6 AM and she slapped the snooze button for another 15 minutes of sleep. She knew her phone was going to ring any time now with Jackson on the other end good morninging her and annoying her just like a brother would. She rolled over and went back to sleep. The alarm and the phone went off at the same time. Still a bit groggy from sleep, she answered the phone.

"Hullo?"

"Good morning, beautiful! How did you sleep?"

Alice sighed. "It is not a good morning. I have to work and I usually get two snoozes before I have to get up. Jackson, you sound like you got your eight hours. Let me get mine."

"Uh, this isn't Jackson. Sorry to have interrupted your beauty sleep. Just wanted to give you the good news. You don't have to work. Jackson and I got someone to fill in for you. Devon was gracious enough to take your shift today, but you'll have to work for her next week."

"Who *is* this?"

"It's Sean, from last night."

Alice groaned and hung up the phone.

Sean stared at the receiver for a full minute before he slowly hung it up. "Well, that's gratitude for ya! She hung up the phone, without saying thank you for getting someone else to work her shift."

Jackson was standing in the corner of the kitchen chortling and trying hard not to choke on his orange juice. "I told you she could be a witch if you woke her up! Did you listen? NO! Did you think because it was YOU calling she would be glad to hear from you? Man, you've been hit in the head too many times!" Jackson snagged a warm biscuit and slathered it with fresh butter. As he stuffed a bite into his mouth, he laughingly told Sean," I'll call her in about half an hour and you can ride with me to get her." Jackson walked away still chuckling at the look on Sean's face.

Half an hour later, Alice's phone rang again. "Good morning, beautiful. Get dressed in the clothes from yesterday. We'll be there to get you in half an hour."

Recognizing Jackson's voice, Alice scrambled out of bed and threw the clothes on from yesterday. Yesterday's clothes meant a trip back to the Baron's and new adventures ahead. She brushed her teeth and thought about taking her hair out of the braid, but decided to just smooth the fine hairs down with some water. She went downstairs to wait so Jackson wouldn't wake anyone else in the dorm with his horn.

When he got there, the passenger door swung open and out stepped Sean, so full of himself that she almost didn't get in the car. He helped her into the back seat while she scowled at both of them during the ride out to the house. Jackson watched her in the rear view while Sean tried to start a conversation with her.

"How did you sleep?" he started, a bit anxious, waiting for her answer.

Alice grunted at him. She saw Jackson's lips quirk, trying to keep from laughing. She raised an eyebrow at him. Whose idea was this anyway? She was starting to get suspicious.

"*Cé an Ifreann a cheapann siad atá á dhúiseacht agam, gan a dhóthain ama a thabhairt dom fiú cupán caife a fháil, agus ansin gníomhú mar is leo féin cad a dhéanfaidh mé agus cé leis a dtéann mé?"* Alice started grousing in Gaelic. Jackson couldn't hide the grin any longer.

"What's she saying?" Sean asked trepidatiously. "Is she gonna kill us?"

Jackson couldn't take it any more. Belly laughing, he tried to explain, "She is not happy with being woken up, especially this early in the morning. She's griping about the fact we didn't even allow time for coffee, and we didn't bring any with us." He couldn't stop laughing.

"Whew! I thought she might be mad at me." Sean wiped imaginary sweat from his brow and slumping back into his seat. He jerked his head around. "Wait, you understood what she just said? You speak that gibberish?"

Alice glared from the back seat. "It's not gibberish! If you had done more research into your persona, you might be able to understand it too. *Fear muc"* she said in Gaelic. She folded her arms across her chest and sat silently the rest of the drive.

That was it. Jackson pulled over to the side of the road and jumped out, choking, from laughing so hard. "Sean, you drive!" he wheezed as he got in on the passenger side.

Sean was still in a state of shock that she used such a vitriolic tone. He slowly got into the driver's seat and continued the drive. Jackson was still chuckling as they pulled up into the driveway. "Pig man? Really?" Choking with laughter, he helped Alice out of the backseat.

The change a night made!! There were tents in the big pasture behind the house. Not just any tents; these were massive in size, like they could hold whole families. All were festooned in the colors of the house that inhabited them.

Then there was the King's tent. A whole platoon of soldiers could sleep inside of it. The coat of arms for His Majesty was emblazoned on the outside: A trio of bears standing upright in the attack position on a field of red. The shields hanging on the entry posts were just as impressive.

Alice stood agape at the hundred people who had mysteriously appeared overnight. Jackson gently took her by the elbow and led her to the kitchen.

"We have to serve this morning. Don't worry," he grinned, "the Baroness will serve the king and his entourage; we get the lesser courtiers."

He put a scarf around his head and she followed his example. After everyone was served, they had a chance to meet up in the kitchen for coffee and a breakfast of their own. They cleared the tables as folks finished their meal and started to wander outside to the field.

The first event was a quest established by the King. The winner was awarded a plaque and a dagger complete with case. The second event was a melee. Peerage against peasants. Alice watched as grown men and women beat each other with rattan sticks and shot padded arrows at each other. The peasants won and the peerage had to ransom the king.

The final event was a huge feast and a ball. Alice was not dressed for the ball, but she enjoyed the feast very much. She tasted grilled quail, mutton, and some of the roasted beef Cassie put on the spit before the sun had come up. Taking her time with the honey mead this time, Alice even enjoyed the music. When most of the folks had wandered off to their beds, Alice asked Jackson to take her back to the dorm.

They thanked their hosts and took their leave. As they got in the car to leave, Sean stood at the door, watching. Alice ignored him. She asked Jackson what Sean's problem was. The whole car ride back, Jackson told her the story of their rivalry.

Sean and Jackson were roommates their first year. Jackson had a girl the first year at college. Sean stole her away, then dumped her. So every time Jackson got a girl, he hastily excluded Alice, Sean would try to schmooze his way into her pants, or leggings as the case might be. Sean did not come back the second year for whatever reason. When they first announced the Quest as their event for the fall, Jackson knew this was something Alice would love, based on his knowledge of her social outings when they were in high school. The first night when she rejected him, Sean was totally dumbfounded that a girl would do that to him. Sean had overheard him sweet talking Devon into taking Alice's shift for the weekend.

He had dialed Alice's number that morning, but Sean, being the arrogant person he was, took the receiver out of Jackson's hand. Jackson tried to tell him to back off, but couldn't help laughing at Sean's reaction when Alice hung up on him. Then when she called him a pig man, the ultimate insult to his obnoxious personality, Jackson chortled at the thought of Sean's face.

Alice reminded Jackson that their relationship was purely platonic, more of a brother and sister. Jackson said he knew, but that was not known in the group. Jackson dropped her at the dorm and waited until she got inside before driving off. Alice sighed. She would be doing quite a bit of research at the library in the morning. She got out her clothes, took a hot shower and crashed.

Her alarm went off at seven on Sunday morning and she rolled out of bed, surprised to find herself stiff and sore. She stretched and jogged down the stairs out to the union for coffee and toast. She headed for the library again and went to the catalog to find what she was looking for. Finding quite a few good references, she went toward the back tables to get a head start on her research. She marked them with a slip from the table and then dug in their indexes to find other references.

She pulled those books and marked them as well. She took the books to check out and went back to her room. Then she started her paper.

Her typewriter chattered and dinged as she documented the items she needed to support her argument. After a few hours she stopped, satisfied this paper would be everything she hoped. This semester was going to be glorious.

Dedication/Intermission page

43

Potty Break Page

Thank you to Wendy for putting up with us and keeping the store open after hours so we can argue about our group name. We appreciate you. Also, thank you for the snacks.

Echoes

By Ada James

Echo: (n) a close parallel or repetition of an idea, feeling, style, or event.
India Evans' pencil scratched harshly across the paper, mirroring the eerie sound of the ice-encased tree limbs scraping against the windows of the old inn. The screeching resembled a cat caught in a wood chipper, sending chills dancing down her spine. On the page, her serial killer, The Archivist, crept up on an isolated inn nestled deep in the countryside, quite similar to the

one she temporarily lived in. He reached into his pocket and fingered the key to the front door as he plowed through shin-deep snow. Soon, he would eliminate yet another family standing in his way.

The bitter cold air bit at her skin despite the wood-burning stove in the room's corner. She pulled the quilt tighter around her shoulders and shivered. The scent of mesquite burning in the fireplace tickled her nose. Holding back a sneeze, she squinted at her paper. Her head ached. Her frozen fingers fumbled the pencil. Flickering candles cast a dim light, making reading after sunset challenging, but deadlines were deadlines. She missed her laptop. *Who knew 'snowpocalypse' would decimate south Texas?*

Ill-equipped to deal with a massive snowstorm, India, her boyfriend, younger brother, grandfather, and half the population of Redus' Crossing descended upon the old inn where at least a fireplace provided warmth and a wood-burning stove allowed cooking.

She squirmed in the red vinyl-seated chair and settled at the rickety formica table. Focus. She stared at the blank page in front of her. The worn wooden floors creaked beneath the heavy boots of people in the next room as they huddled around the roaring hearth. A quiet murmur of conversation served as background noise to her writing. *Not my normal playlist, but it'll do. It'll do.*

An image of the cranky innkeeper crossed her mind, wrinkled and grumpy. *At least someone was profiting from the downed power grid. The woman was charging a surcharge per cord of wood consumed. Crazy old bat would have burned the wood to keep herself warm.* She glanced at her manuscript; the words waiting to be written. She tapped her pencil against her lips, chewing on the eraser absentmindedly. *Maybe she should be my next victim.*

A quiet moment passed, followed by another, as India contemplated the next move in her story. She continued writing, her thoughts flowing from the pencil onto the page. The Archivist, a mysterious figure from her novel, slipped through the front door, his presence shrouded in darkness. A scream echoed from the foyer as his blade kissed the neck of the cantankerous innkeeper.

There, she thought, *that will teach the hag.* Steam rose from the hot blood, swirling in the air before it splashed across the worn wooden floor, pooling in front of the door. What an image. At least India assumed it made a brilliant image. Sometimes dealing with aphantasia made her job as an author twice as hard. Although with the dark images her words created, perhaps not seeing was a blessing in disguise.

Lost in her imaginary world, India started as the kitchen door creaked open. Footsteps echoed on the hardwood floors, the sound growing louder, closer. A shadow fell over the page, casting a chilling presence. Wrapped up in her story, she leaped to her feet, her heart racing with a mix of excitement and fear. She had just written this exact scenario in her novel. If life followed her words, in the next few seconds, a knitted scarf pulled tight around her neck would cut off her ability to breathe.

Pulse galloping, she spun around, her pencil poised to stab her attacker. "Grandda." She blew out a heavy breath and dropped back into her chair. Placing a trembling hand on her chest, she tried to steady her zooming heart. It thundered beneath her palm. With a shaky laugh, she dropped the pencil, letting it clatter against the formica tabletop. "A little warning next time, could ya?"

Her grandfather chuckled, the rich, deep sound filling the room. "Still on a crusade to write the future?" He tapped his cigarette package against the side of his hand, shaking loose a smoke. "Aye, your ma and her ma before her had a touch of the sight, but none can control the flow of time." He winked. "Or can they?"

"Not in here. You know the rules."

Her grandfather's playful expression morphed into one of pleading. "Come now, lass, you wouldn't be sending an auld man into this wicked storm, now would ye? Ye'd be sending me to me death."

"It's not much colder outside than it is in here. And I'm surviving." She tipped her head to the side and cast a considering glance at her grandfather. "Or you could always do without the cigarette?"

"*Mo chridhe*, did I ever tell you about the ice storm of 1888? The year of the three fat ladies, it was."

Frustration swamped India. The ticking of the clock became more pronounced. She heard her deadline creeping closer. "Grandda, am I honestly supposed to believe you were alive 150 years ago? Why do you always call it the year of the three fat ladies? Do you know how insulting that is?"

"Insulting?" He scooped the pencil from the tabletop and wrote 1888 in his elegant, looping handwriting. "Look at it, child. Do you not see the sensuous curves? Pleasingly voluptuous lasses, how can that be an insult?"

Her shoulders slumped, weighed down by defeat. A heavy sigh escaped her lips as she whispered, "I surrender." *Might as well. Grandda always won. I wish I had inherited his gift of gab instead of just the ability to capture emotion with words on the page.* "But no smoking inside. You know you shouldn't be smoking at all."

A throbbing headache pulsed in her temples as she mustered the strength to stand. She stomped over to the refrigerator. With a reproachful glance at her grandfather, she jerked the door open. Even with no electricity, the appliance stayed cold.

Carrots? Cookie dough? She peered over her shoulder as her much younger brother whirled into the room, waving his iPad in the air. The sound of his excited voice filled the air, competing with her pounding head. *Cookie dough it is.*

With the bowl of dough and a spoon in hand, she stalked back to the kitchen table. She dropped into her chair and shoved a spoonful of the treat into her mouth, the familiar flavor of chocolate soothing her. She retrieved her pencil. If she didn't get this story to her editor by the end of the week, she could kiss her career goodbye.

"India," her brother whined, his twelve-year-old voice desperate for attention. "Did you hear a word I said? Your stories are coming true." He thrust the iPad towards her, the screen illuminating his worried face.

She swept her hair from her face. She picked up the stack of papers in front of her and waved them in the air. "Ryan, working, deadline. Remember?" She shook the papers in his direction. "You like to eat, don't you?"

"Sister, please. Stop writing." Fear tinged his words. He shoved his tablet in her face. "People are dying. You are killing them."

The weight of his words hung in the air, casting a shadow over her determined resolve. She couldn't ignore the urgency in his voice, the fear in his eyes. Her grip on the pencil loosened. A slight tremor ran through her hand. Rubbing her temples, she squinted at the flickering screen of the tablet. *How does this thing still have power?* The dim glow illuminated the headline that made her heart race: "Archivist Strangles Co-eds." *That can't be real. The Archivist doesn't exist. I made him up.*

Ryan navigated to another website. "Family of five murdered. Father found near front door. Throat slit."

The sickening odor of fear permeated the air, competing with the scent of unbaked cookie dough. Bile rushed up the back of India's throat. The cookie dough threatened to reappear. Each detail from her story appeared in a recent news headline. *What have I done?*

The front door creaked open. A gust of frigid wind blew the pages of her unfinished story to the floor. From the foyer, a high-pitched scream dissolved into a wet, gasping gurgle. The sounds of a violent struggle followed, punctuated by her boyfriend's panicked cries. The jarring sound of a gunshot silenced his warning mid-cry.

A tall, imposing figure stood in the doorway, silhouetted against the dim glow of the setting sun reflecting on the snow outside. The sharp gleam of a menacing machete dangled from one hand, while the other hand clutched the cold metal of a pistol. India grabbed her brother by the shoulders, her nails digging into his flesh. She shoved him toward Grandda, desperation etched across her face. "Run!" she screamed.

Ryan stumbled forward, his widened eyes reflecting sheer terror. His body quaked, his legs locked into place.

India exchanged a knowing glance with her aged grandfather. A grim expression passed between them. They both understood the stakes.

Grandda nodded solemnly. This was her fight, and they both knew it. His duty was to protect Ryan. Hers was to stop the monster she had created.

Turning to face the intruder, India's heart pounded in her chest as her eyes widened in fear. The dimly lit room seemed to close in on her, adding to her sense of impending doom. India swallowed hard. The bitter, metallic tang of adrenaline flooded her mouth, numbing her tongue.

If she failed to eliminate him, she would lose everything: her brother, her grandfather, her life. The weight of guilt for all the others already gone swamped her soul, suffocating her with regret. Pushing the feeling aside, she moved quickly. Hands trembling, she scooped up the pages of her unfinished manuscript and darted around the dark figure.

He grabbed for her; his fingers brushed against her arm.

She evaded his grasp. With a swift motion, she flung the pages into the crackling fire, igniting a shower of sparks that danced in the air like fireflies. The room filled with the scent of burning paper, acrid smoke, and her own fear-soaked sweat.

An unholy shriek pierced the air, drowning out the crackling of the fire and the thud of her pulse in her ears. The shadow man vanished as if he had never existed at all.

India collapsed to her knees, the floor hard and cold beneath them. *Gone. Once and for all.*

***

Tessa stood and bent forward, stretching the muscles of her back. A pop-pop-pop sound filled the room as she rolled her neck on her shoulders. *Ugh. That last bit needs rewritten. It happens too fast. How does India know burning the pages will defeat the bad guy?* She scribbled a note to herself on the pad sitting beside her laptop. She glanced at the blue-green digital numbers on the microwave. *Crap! Eight a.m. I'm going to be late for work—again.*

Slamming her laptop closed, her footsteps echoed through the hallway as she darted into the bedroom to grab clothing before rushing into the bathroom. Hot steam scented with soothing eucalyptus filled the room as she opened the hot shower tap all the way.

Never had a story consumed her this way before. The weight of exhaustion settled in her bones, a testament to the sleepless night she had spent pouring herself onto the pages. *I can't believe I stayed up all night writing.*

Stepping from the shower, Tessa's skin tingled with the sensation of warmth contrasting with the cool air in the room. She wrapped the soft towel tighter around her body as gooseflesh raised on her arms. Hollering down the hallway, her voice echoed, bouncing off the walls. "Hon? Why'd you let me stay up all night like that?"

No response.

Still wrapped in the fuzzy towel, Tessa dashed to the bedroom, leaving a trail of wet footsteps in her path. "Hon?" She peered into the empty bedroom, her eyes scanning for any signs of movement. The room seemed void of life, its emptiness casting a shadow over her thoughts. *That's weird.*

Trying to shake off her increasing sense of dread, she approached the front windows. A cool draft snuck around the frame. She peeked outside. *Huh.*

Jake's sleek silver Dodge truck sat in the neatly paved driveway, its metallic gleam reflecting the sunlight. Parked beside it, Tessa's Jeep mirrored its glow. She grinned. She loved the fact that they chose matching colors for their vehicles. It was the little things that kept their romance alive. Little things like him choosing their anniversary as their postal box number. She smiled as the memory danced across her mind.

The postmistress held out two keys. "I have box 928 or 1013 available."

Without hesitation, Jake snatched the key to 928 from the postmistress's hand, a mischievous grin spreading across his face as he winked at Tessa. His playful words melted her heart. "We'll take this one. I'll never forget our anniversary as long as I remember our address."

Tessa felt bad. She hadn't even made the correlation between the post office box number and the date. What kind of romance writer was she, anyway? *Well, technically, I don't write romance. Not yet, at least.*

She grimaced as she thought of the last attempt she had made at writing romance. A simple, clean, sweet love story—all her writer friends assured her it would be easy. *Easy, my ass. Within the first four chapters, she had included a stalking, a kidnapping, an arson, and murder. Yeah, real easy.*

She shook her head to clear her thoughts. "Jake, honey? Where are you?"

The wooden floor in the next room creaked. "Jake? Is that you?" A tremor of fear danced down her spine. *Stop it. Just because you write scary things is no reason to believe scary things are in your home. It's fiction, remember. Just like you told Mom when she wondered where she had gone wrong raising you.*

Silence answered her call. She couldn't shake the unease. With cautious steps, she tip-toed to the doorway. Gulping down a breath to stay quiet, she peered around the frame into the hallway. Her eyes widened in horror as they fell upon a trail of rust-colored drops soiled the cream-colored carpet. A trail that led to a dark silhouette crouched over Jake's motionless form.

A bloodcurdling scream escaped Tessa's throat, reverberating through the air. Panic surged through her veins, urging her to flee. She turned to run, but before she made it over two steps, an ice-cold hand wrapped around her throat, lifting her feet from the floor and shoving her against the wall. The hand squeezed tighter and tighter. Darkness enveloped her vision, leaving her struggling to breathe.

***

Oh, that's good. I leisurely stretched my tired muscles, the satisfying pull and release reinvigorating me. I reached for the coffee mug sitting beside my keyboard. Its warmth seeped into my fingers. I brought the cup closer to my lips and inhaled the rich aroma of the luxurious hot cocoa waiting inside the mug. As the velvety liquid caressed my tongue, a contented sigh escaped me. A symphony of flavors danced on my palate.

Lost in my thoughts, I pondered what might come next. The unfinished plot tugged at me. *I can't leave it like that. All those echoes.*

I set my cocoa aside and returned my fingers to the keyboard, ideas dancing around my mind. Focusing on just one was like herding cats. A sudden noise shattered the tranquility of my surroundings.

Startled, my gaze darted toward my closed office door. *I'm here alone. Unless Cregg came home early.* I peeked out the curtains. A sigh of relief slipped past my lips. His jeep sat in the driveway. "Darlin', you're home early. Everything okay at the office?"

No answer.

"Darlin'? You okay?"

Still no answer.

My heart throbbed in my chest like a bird of prey attempting to escape a cage. "Cregg, this isn't funny. Answer me."

A chilling sensation crawled up my spine as my eyes locked onto the doorknob, which rotated slowly. The door creaked open, one slow inch at a time. Dim light filtered through the doorway and revealed a haunting silhouette, casting an eerie shadow against the walls. The figure stood motionless, filling the frame with an intimidating presence.

My senses heightened. The smell of hot iron danced on the cool breeze. I could almost taste the metallic tang of blood that dripped from the menacing machete clutched in the intruder's hand. Each droplet fell with a haunting rhythm, echoing against the polished hardwood floor. Always echoing.

The Archivist.

Up in Smoke

By Tess Monroe

On your couch you sit, I am with you.

Looking around, your memories are everywhere.

I was there. The beach, the barbeque, the birthdays. I went too.

Then divorce, broken dreams and drinking. I witnessed it all.

From good days to the worst, I helped you come through.

Here we sit. What's on your mind?

Here you sit. Reeling over time.

What to do? Come on, nothing to lose.

There you go, a steady pace.

This I know wins the race.

What started as fun, cannot be undone.

One here, one there. In secret and pair.

Look at us now! Did you think you were immune?

I mean you haven't cared.

You tried to quit. I called you back. Your willpower cracked.

Here we sit. This is your future.

Oxygen readings and a clean suture.

Here you sit unable to do. Here I sit waiting for you.

Go on! Come on! Let's have a little fun! That's it! That's it! Light just one!

Cut the flow of air from your umbilical cord. One more cigarette you can afford.

Just like that, my crusade is done.

Here I sit. I've done what I came to do.

Burning at one end to help you.

Here you sit. Unable to breathe. Filling your lungs, I watch you heave.

One day soon there will be no you. Just me. No I.

But for now. Let's sit and smoke a bit.

The Great Vape Crusades

By Caitlyn Lasater
Art by Briley Blanchard

SmokeSphereSocial Post:
The Great Vape Crusades: a Historical Record
Uploaded by Zachariah Zimmelzyn, III (@ZachluvsZynnie)

This is a once-upon-a-time story, but only because it was once in time and upon a small embankment, not because it is a classic story opener. And, once upon a time is a much better qualifiable opener than anything else I've discovered in my myriad of internet searches, so it's just that.

Once upon a time, a mushroom—the exploding, radiant sort—brought death and destruction and a few other choice alliteration descriptors; however, strangely enough, it also brought life. For, according to a lovely chap by the name of Newton, every action has an equal and opposite reaction. Therefore, it simply makes sense that, if death happens, so does life. Natural conclusions for a natural event, you see.

Anywho, because of Newton and his machinations, life appeared after the great mushroom eradicated everything else. Much like the unwanted dandelions after a lawn is freshly mowed, the drudges of society reared their ugly butts—yes, butts, you'll see why momentarily, don't fret—to the sky and grew a human-like consciousness. Or at least, a consciousness that is verifiably close to human, if any science men were still around to verify such things.

Oh, I digress though. You'll find this is a common trope in my writings. Forgive me, as it's difficult to write without arms. Or fingers. Or a functioning nervous system. The point I'm trying to make here, in case you aren't picking up what I'm putting down, is that I'm trying my best, just like those cheeky little butts.

And yes, that was a pun. Thank you for noticing. I worked hard at it.

Now, those aforementioned butts go by another name: les cigarettes! Yes, yes. The lowly cigarette became sentient after the sudden burst of radiation that doused half of the planet and torched the rest. Don't ask me how that happened, but it did. The cigarettes became living, but not breathing, creatures. They rose from derelict ashtrays, moldy gutters, and overgrown grass behind questionable bars to peer and gaze in wonder at the ever red sky with tiny little faces and tiny little eyeses and tiny little mouthses. But not tiny little noses because they don't breathe and honestly that's probably for the best because who wants to smell cigarettes all day?

However, alongside the cigarettes, there came another. Just one other (is this starting to sound a little bit like a franchise with a ring or twenty? I hope that's not copyrighted. My agent won't be happy). Well, and me I suppose. I'm not certain I really count though in the grand scheme of it all, as I am merely documenting the course of history for future generations, however long it may take for the current ocean blobs to gain language. It took what—a few million years last time to grow a single brain cell? I can wait. I'm stocked up on books. Oh, sorry. I'm doing it again, aren't I? Let's see, ah yes. Alongside the cigarettes, this other-not-me emerged from hidden pockets in teenagers' rooms, from the various drawers of college students, school bathroom pipes and ceilings, and stores that pandered to the youth and those undergoing their middle life crisis. Plastic and metal, the smooth, sleek, and stylish vapes awoke, took one look at the burnt out butts, and immediately declared themselves superior.

See? I told you they had a human conscience.

Now you must understand that cigarettes and vapes, though similar, are very, very different. For your comfort, I have provided a handy Venn diagram:

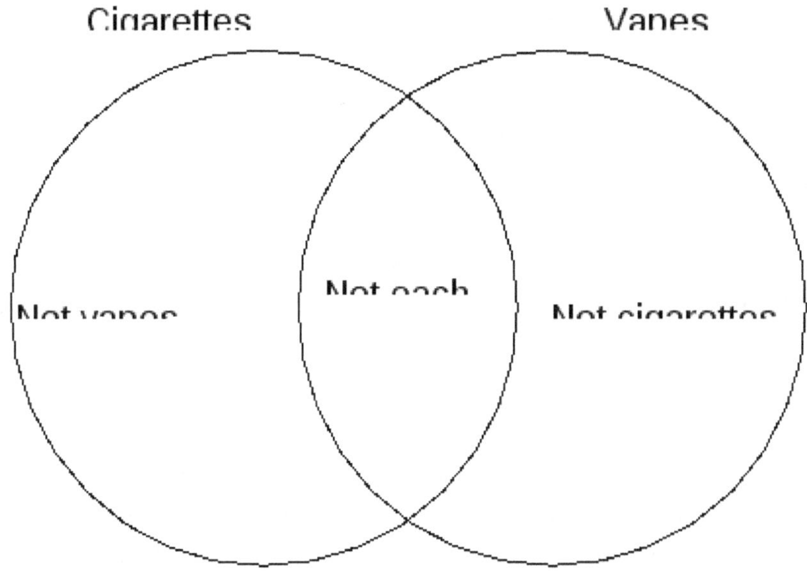

Hopefully this diagram has helped to clear up any misconceptions about the two. I know I was confused at first as I watched from my plastic "Diet Coke" prison that torments me daily. I have a rather funny anecdote about mistaking a cigarillo and an elf bar, but—

No, no. I must stick to the plan!

Back to the differences....as you can see, they are numerous. And the cigarettes and vapes are well aware of these differences, too. So the sophisticated, streamlined, and smart-looking vapes put the cigarettes to work.

Now, armless and legless though I am, I am not brainless. I know what you're asking: why am I still devoting precious minutes of my mortal life to this nonsense? I can assure you, I asked myself this same thing (minus the mortality bit) each time I manage to write a letter with my potent psychic abilities (and by that I mean the pen nib I managed to work into a hole in my side in order to scribble on the inside of this bottle). For that, I have no answers other than an imaginary shoulder shrug.

For your second rumination though, I do have a response: the vapes are very convincing. One could even say they are addictive. They managed to persuade the cigarettes in a, ah, unique manner.

The cunning vapes told the cigarettes that they needed their infinite wisdom, playing on the concept that cigarette butts last anywhere between eighteen months to ten years in the wilderness. The vapes don't last more than a day or two without needing to be recharged or requiring a replacement cartridge. They were hopefully recycled, but based on the number of vapes that came crawling from the sewers, clearly they were tossed like greasy food after a night of heavy drinking. The vapes pleaded for the cigarettes' help to exist themselves.

As for why the cigarettes listened? Well, my undergrad is in Psychology, and I'll fill you in (for free) on a little tidbit that you must *swear* to never use for nefarious purposes. Swear? Okay, good. It's a well-known psychological trick that asking someone for a favor makes them like you more! Yes, it seems a bit counter-intuitive, but it works. Trust me. It's got something to do with feeling trusted or accepted by the person asking the favor. Personally, I've concluded it's more likely that it appeals to people's God-complex and affirms the line of thinking that they're superior in every way to the person doing the asking.

Or maybe that's just me.

Regardless (and please stop saying irregardless, that's incorrect and gives me a nervous tic), just as the vapes intended, the cigarettes were more than happy to do their best to haul the vapes to and from their charging stations.

And yes, they maintained power. You'd think they wouldn't what with the complete eradication of the planet–except of course the cigarettes, the vapes, and your very reliable narrator–but the vapes, having been manufactured with fanciness in mind, resorted to fanciness themselves.

All it took was a hamster wheel, a battery, some wires, cigarettes with makeshift legs and arms and ta-da! Power. Or something like that. I'm fairly positive that's how they made it work at least, but I unfortunately skipped physics the day we learned about circuitry, so I could be wrong. There's definitely a wheel involved, though. I can see them running on it right now.

Regardless (See? Proper use, people!), the vapes taught the cigarettes how to generate electricity in order to keep the rechargeable ones nice and animate. And the rechargeable ones looked down their not-noses at the cheaper, less-spiffy disposable vapes and said, (I'm going to paraphrase here for liability reasons) "Sure, you're vapes, but you're not *vapes*—what happens when you run out of juice, my dear? You're obsolete! Not much better than a plastic cigarette in that regard, are you, love?"

And of course the disposable vapes initially argued that–I mean, I would argue it too if someone said I was little more than cigarette guts in a bag–but the very convincing rechargeable vapes simply ignored their protestations. What could they do? I mean, they used all their juice arguing and keeled over.

Now, if we know anything, what is it that we know? Besides that Pluto is a planet and I will die before I declare there aren't nine planets in our solar system, we know that exclusionary practices breed discontent. And–remember the human consciousness!—discontent breeds malice.

Unless, of course, you give them cake.

Well, figuratively. Obviously, neither vapes nor cigarettes give a flying fiddle about cake. Why would they need cake? We've established they only need electricity. And, if they did need cake for some odd reason, well that's just too bad. There isn't any. All the cake is gone. Poof. I mean literally poof. After the hoarding and limiting water supply, you couldn't get water for the batter anyways, regardless of the mushroom. And don't get me started on the eggs. Hello, bird flu anyone? Haha, I crack (like an egg! Get it?) myself up!

Oh, sorry. I did it again, didn't I? Drat. Yes, so, ah, after the wars over water, and the mushroom, cake is permanently off the menu and has become nothing but a sweet metaphor and allusion combination by me. But the point still stands.

The rechargeable vapes gave the disposable vapes metaphorical and ~~allusitory~~ (is that a word? What's the adjective for allusion? A moment, please) *allusive* cake: the disposable vapes were tasked with overseeing the cigarettes! Yes, it's much easier to accept your lot in life if you can bully others! For exam

Oh, dear, dear! I'm so sorry to end in the middle of a paragraph like that. How unprofessional of me. I suddenly found myself lacking for writing room on the inside of my bottle. I managed to throw myself against the wall of the bottle enough times to render it sideways. This was favorable, but I must say the ten feet of rolling after was not. After being violently ill from the spinning, I managed to use the pen nib as a makeshift piton to drag myself to the cigarette and vape city–formerly known as Cigarette and Vape City–and found a lovely new bottle to write in. This one is glass and somewhat opaque and faintly smells of bad decisions, but it will have to do. I must admit it is an excellent vantage point to the city.

Where was I? Oh, yes. So the disposable vapes oversee the cigarette's work on behalf of the rechargeable vapes. We now have a social hierarchy not unlike that of corporate. Please see the diagram below to help with understanding the hierarchy:

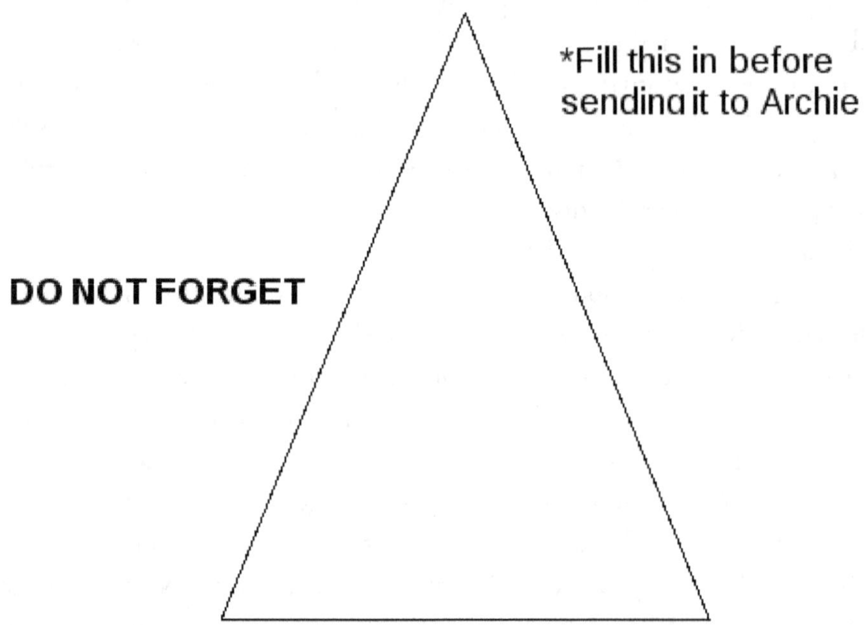

Much like the now-evaporated unpaid interns, the cigarettes toil away to complete back-breaking, menial labor for the vapes for imaginary cake for free.

And it's really not like the labor is easy. Have you ever tried to plug a charger into a wall with tiny paper hands? I haven't but from this bottle I can watch the cigarettes do it and all I can say is I'm quite happy with my pen nub hole instead. Who knows what terrors those smooth, succulent, silky vapes would enact on my fragile, fabric body! Ah, I feel faint at just the notion of such brutality. They would probably use me for a pillow! And, well, I just can't have that. Hence, my need for the bottles.

Ah drat. I've done it again. Oh, well. The tangents give me plot filler to complete my essay length requirement. Not that I need plot filler, I mean. I've got plenty of plot. All the plot. The plottiest plot that's ever been plotted.

So, now that we have discussed that I definitely do not need plot filler, let us continue with the history. So far, we have the vapes and cigarettes coming to life after a mushroom graced us with its presence and then the vapes decided that the cigarettes were only worth menial labor to keep them working and well charged and they also decided that there were two kinds of vapes and then the disposable vapes were mad but the rechargeable vapes let them be the bosses of the menial labor performing cigarettes. Glad we have that covered.

And this continued for a long time. How long? I would wager it took at least four hours. When you're a vape, cigarette, or me, that's a lifetime. Like when they say that flies live an entire lifetime in twenty-four hours because of their tiny size, but different because I am not a fly.

So the cigarettes did all the hard work while the vapes, essentially, did nothing. They did the managerial work. And that's not to say that managers aren't important (please don't put my historical document down if you're a manager and I've offended you, I've got six kids!) but that is to say that after a time, the cigarettes became....disgruntled. As they should. You know they only have little arms to use because they had to peel down their papery skin to make crinkly appendages, right? Would you be thrilled if someone flayed you and made you use the skin ribbons for pampering them? No? Didn't think so. And if you're trying to be edgy by saying yes, you're lying and stop it.

Now, there are a few ways disgruntled cigarettes handle their business. The first one is they gather at the water cooler and make small talk that invariably leads to a conversation about how they would run things if they were in charge–this in turn leads to them saying 'too many chiefs and too few Indians' even though that saying is not politically correct (please let me know if you have a better analogy that is not offensive). Then, when a disposable vape comes by, they hush and begin to discuss the sudden drop on the DOW.

And, in case you're wondering how I know what they're saying, communication is done through smoke signals these days. We don't have vocal cords–well, some of the rechargeable vapes can make a beep sound–so that's how it's done. I must communicate solely through writing as I lack the ability to produce vapor or smoke.

Unless I light myself on fire.

And I don't think I'd like to do that.

Easily translated, the smoke signals around the water cooler grew more and more frazzled as the days went by. They began to talk of unionizing, but a vape quickly shut that down by saying their wages would be docked. One cigarette pointed out they didn't have wages, and the vape told them that was besides the point. I found myself disagreeing here, but the cigarettes nodded their little burnt heads and agreed with the vape, oddly enough.

After the union plan fell through, one brave cigarette suggested that maybe one of them apply for a senior level position that was recently opened, as Victor Vaperson, D.V., recently ran out of juice. A few puffs of agreement ran around and then, right before my very eyes, that very brave cigarette rolled to the rechargeable vapes and asked for an application.

I would like to pause here to say I do not promote bullying before continuing the story.

The rechargeable vapes laughed, pointed, and laughed some more at the cigarette (well, they tried to laugh. I've heard vaping can be bad for your lungs) and dismissed them without so much as an interview promise. I do understand that the cigarette did not follow appropriate protocol by not sending in an application, but goodness gracious, to audaciously laugh seems a bit inappropriate. Improper office etiquette. If I were that cigarette, I would march my way to HR and make a report.

And, as you can imagine, the cigarette did not like the crusty, rusty wannabe laughing from the vapes. No, they did not like that at all. So much so, that this little cigarette hatched a plan.

Normally I would also suggest that this cigarette's plan be mentioned to HR at the least (and potentially the police because murder is wrong), but honestly? They kind of deserve it. And I know I'm supposed to be an unbiased observer but I would be lying if I said I didn't give a tiny little imaginary air pump when I first saw that completed smoke signal communique. If I had arms, I would have probably high fived something. Alas, some joys are never to be discovered.

Would you like to know what the plan was? No? Oh. Well. I wasn't expecting that answer honestly.

This is embarrassing. If I had thumbs, I would twiddle them. Maybe avert my gaze a bit and blush. Or maybe I would cry.

Please, just give me a moment to compose myself.

I've thought it over and I've decided that I'm going to tell you anyway. We all must learn things we have no interest in in order to be good, upstanding citizens—taxes come to mind. Nobody likes them, but we must learn them. So you shall gain this knowledge regardless of your personal protestations. Much like an algebra teacher, I shall pour the knowledge into your head. What you choose to do with said knowledge is up to you. Blank stare all you like, but it's going to happen.

The smoke signals spelled out a simple question: what if we didn't charge them?

Whispers abounded.

"They'll extinguish us!"

"But they need our help!"

"What did they say? I'm a slow reader!"

"We can't kill them!"

The cigarette assuaged their bombardment. "It's not killing them. We help them. And what do we get?"

"We get to experience the joy that altruism brings!"

Please allow me to describe the cigarette's face to you with an emoji, a nifty expression created by typical writing symbols:

‾.‾

Isn't it adorable?

The cigarette put his noseless face in his paper strip hands and made a puff of smoke that can only be described as an annoyed sigh. The cigarette put it to a vote. And, surprise surprise, nobody else wanted to kill the vapes out of fear of being indicted. Of course, I don't need to point out that the judicial system collapsed alongside society, but how could these poor, primitive cigarettes know such a thing? Their society was behind a rusty old bar that was, in its heyday, still a rusty old bar. My intuition tells me that many poor decisions that began with my current writing space ended with the judicial system in that bar.

Actually, come to think of it, they should be legal experts. Maybe they'd be willing to offer me a free consultation on how I can get half of the house from Zynobia before our divorce is settled. I'll have to ask. Archie, remind me before publication.

Anywho, the lone cigarette was now outnumbered by his law-abiding peers. And, as with all revolutions, it fizzled out. Having given up to the hierarchy imposed upon them and enforced by laws that protect only the powerful, the cigarettes continued to grumble at their water cooler and waste away charging the vapes via hamster wheel.

I would like to take a moment here to give a brief history lesson. Alexander the Great was potentially buried alive. Yes, tragic isn't it? To be cut down in your prime by a paralysis disease only for your friends to put you in a tomb and leave you there while you slowly perish, completely mentally aware of everything, down to the last breath leaving your body...

Also, the American Revolution and the French Revolution. They both had ideas that stemmed from the unfair treatment of the populace by the few "elite" and ended with a new society being born, one that was based on equality. I'm sure you see where I'm going with this.

But in case you don't, I'll tell you: REVOLUTION! THE GLORIOUS REVOLUTION!!

You see, that clever little cigarette smoldered rather than allowing their dream to completely fizzle out. And one day, at the water cooler, that cigarette was informed that they lost their job come the next thirty minutes. Though the cigarette begged and pleaded, the disposable vape reminded them that the cigarettes are only useful as long as they are able to burn and use their arms, and this cigarette was approaching the end of its lifespan. You'd think they would offer a retirement program or a pension of some sort, but no. This is actually all too common. Firing someone before retirement so that pensions don't have to be paid out—predatory practices in general—but to do it to this poor, sad little cigarette? This poor, scheming little cigarette?

Well, the cigarette simply refused to plug in the rechargeable vape. Yep. That cigarette marched to the hamster wheel battery rig and simply grabbed the cord and...dropped it.

Oh I wish you were there to see it. It was stunning. Picture it: the decrepit bar, the burnt out skeletons, the incinerated sky, and the gaping mouths of the vapes and cigarettes alike. I must say, the next moments were the chef's kiss. Not that chefs should be doing any kissing as that's a health hazard, but it's a common phrase known as an idiom. Just clarifying for you. If you're a chef, please don't partake in any kissing on the job. It's unsanitary and I may have to call in that free consultation from the legal team behind the bar. Meaning the cigarettes. Because earlier I mentioned they may have a firm grasp of the law. You know what? Just, just edit that bit out Archie. Thanks.

Ah, where were we? Oh yes. Just picture it: the decrepit bar, the burnt out skeletons, the incinerated sky, and the gaping mouths of the vapes and cigarettes. And me.

The rechargeable vape whose cord was dropped vaped out, "Pick it up!" And the cigarette, that brave, poor, scheming, sad, and smart cigarette? They puffed, "Do it yourself." Then they waggled their little paper arms as a reminder to the vapes that they were indeed armless.

It was incredible. Right up until a vape extinguished the cigarette with a puff of water vapor and kicked the corpse down the tiny sludge river that flowed behind the bar, but up until that point it was incredible. Then it was a little macabre. I may or may not have once again been ill, having just witnessed a murder. Weirdly enough, the vapes don't seem to worry about killing their workers, but the cigarettes seem to worry about killing their bosses. Hm. It's almost as if the top level can get away with things if they just say "Oh, I sneezed and blew out their flame, it was a tragic, tragic accident! I'll be sure to give their family the life insurance policy." I mean the cigarette legal team didn't really argue much. They just started plugging in the charging cords as fast as they could. They ran even faster on the hamster wheel. All while the corpse (well, mostly butt now) disappeared with the sludge flow.

I really thought that would be it. I watched for a few more hours, and nothing. Nothing, I say! The cigarettes toiled on as usual, and the vapes did nothing as usual. I was so certain that the GLORIOUS REVOLUTION would happen.

Disappointment is a hard pill to swallow, despite the fact I have no idea what a pill is. But what could I do? I couldn't leave. That would be giving up my research! Besides, I'd hate to think what they would do to me if they caught me in this bottle. Forget being a pillow, they'd probably make me tap dance and I haven't taken tap dancing class since I was five. Add that to my stage fright, and it's going to be a nightmare all around that will undoubtedly end with me being shaken out for my guts and then my frail, fabric skin being tossed into the sludge.

Actually, I think I'm going to lay low for a while. Just, uh, give me some time. There may be a sequel here somewhere. But for now, I think I will try to roll this bottle elsewhere.

Be sure to like and subscribe for any updates. Archie, direct them to my channel, please. Remember, you get ten percent.

Dad GUMMIT! It happened. Pardon my language, but it happened and I missed it!! Based on the looks of things, the cigarettes are in full revolt—I want to say things began at the water cooler as it's tipped over, but I missed it—I was definitely not ruminating on my ex wife and what I could have done better (sure, I could have taken out the trash a little more and made sure to take in some of the mental load, but I was a good spouse, I swear it! Zynobia, if you're reading this, come back! I'll change, I swear!) because I was most assuredly having my view blocked by a bit of acid rain. Yes, acid rain. That's it. I had to uh, move my bottle to get a better view and I missed the inciting incident.

The cigarettes are now tearing chargers from the hamster wheel. A few of them have actually banded together at its base and are—wow! They're pushing it! They've managed to topple it over! And now, with their paper arms raised, they're rushing the vapes. They spray their vapor and, sadly, dozens of the cigarettes go down, their little flames fading into nothingness.

Please, I need a moment.

This is so difficult to watch. The cigarettes are overwhelming the vapes, and they are now ripping the disposable ones apart and drinking their juice. I'm all for the GLORIOUS REVOLUTION, but I'm not sure how I feel about

Well, it's not really cannibalism is it? I mean, they're different species. It's a bit like if a human ate a chimp. Weird, but not cannibalistic. So what to call it then? I suppose predation works according to my search, but it feels much more personal than simply predation. I'll invent a new word. Let's call it cousinanibalism. I'd like to think we are cousins on the evolutionary tree, so that's going to be the new term.

The cigarettes are engaging in cousinanibalism—so much juice. They're painting their butts with it. Licking it up with their tiny mouthses. And it's...it's making them stronger, I think. They're burning brighter. They're running faster. And now they're at the rechargeable vapes.

Oh dear, one was just speared through with the prongs of its charger. That's...something. You know, I really thought I was ready for this. All my careful watching and planning and documentation. But I mean, I really think they could have approached this better. Maybe petitioned or held it to a vote. However, as a historian I must recognize that many great battles and GLORIOUS REVOLUTIONS only happened with violence. And, as long as it's for a just cause, I suppose it must be imaginary-stomached. And, based on the evidence above, I'll let you make the judgment call on whether or not this is a just GLORIOUS REVOLUTION. You seem rather entranced by my documentation, or at least I hope you are if you've made it this far in the histories. Maybe you're reading it for class and you're not actually interested in anything other than a good grade, which I'm proud of you for wanting, but I'd really prefer it if someone enjoyed my work for the sake of wanting to learn more about the…I'll call it the Great Vape Crusades.

Oh, it seems the cigarettes just tied the last remaining vapes together with a charging cord and set them atop the river. They are currently busy gathering bone fragments and a bit of fabric—I hope that's not from a fellow researcher—and they are making a raft from the vapes. No, a sailboat.

Other cigarettes are gathering bottle caps and glass fragments. They're making them into battle axes and shields? I swear, one even has a tiny helmet with horns. Wildly inaccurate, but I must presume they're much better at the law than they are knowing the historical record concerning Viking raiders.

And there they go. Off to right the world in their little boat. Is…is this how empty nesters feel? I am so proud. What do I do with myself now? Oh, I hope the sludge river doesn't chew through the hull. I'd imagine that is not very comfortable for the vapes on the bottom.

You know, I was going to use this as a sort of allegory for not taking advantage of the working class, but I don't think I can condone using the bodies of those who have wronged you as a sailboat hull. That just seems a tad too much. So uh, maybe let's just look at this instead as a lovely little tale about making friends. We are friends now.

Congratulations.

But also, don't take advantage of the cigarettes. Or do and give me another historical record to document.

Thanks.

I'll follow the raft as soon as I can find a way to make my bottle airtight and overcome my hydrophobia, and I'll update you on the Great Vape Crusades.

About the Authors

Heather Schrader is the founder and teacher of Heather's Cottage School in Texas. She is passionate about teaching English and mathematical literacy, scientific exploration, and theological application. When not teaching she enjoys many creative outlets such as writing, painting, jewelry, and candle making. Heather has her B.A. in Elementary Education with a Studio Art concentration and over 20 years' experience teaching in and out of the classroom. She and her husband enjoy the variety of students, piles of books, plants, cats, dogs, birds, reptiles, amphibians, and adventures God brings their way.

∞

Johnathon Dagger. He questions everything, especially why he questions everything. He stole his name from his teenage best friend's Nom de Plume because he wasn't using it anyway. In addition to his technical and entrepreneurial pursuits, Johnathon is a contributing author to Generator Five, the first anthology by the Atascosa Writers Group. His storytelling reflects his connections to the community and his desire to share its narratives with a broader audience. When he's not developing software or helping his wife run their bookstore, Jonathan enjoys crafting stories that resonate with readers, exploring the real and imagined highways at the intersection of technology, history, and human experience.

∞

From the COVID-induced virtual college graduation came a woman who, despite the insistent desire to recluse from society, now finds herself writing a sci-fi thriller short story contributing to the first ever Atascosa Writer's Group Anthology. Writing, like carbonated drinks, coffee, and collecting cosmetics, is **Amanda Minniear**'s passion. She typically writes various forms of poetry but is excited to showcase her unique approach to creative writing in this collaborative project.

∞

A lover of dragon tales and fantasy romance, **Michaelle Shingleton** was born in Biloxi, MS and moved to Texas over 30 years ago. She is currently employed in the oil field as an executive administrative assistant. Her love of the printed word was instilled at an early age by her parents who not only encouraged it, but practiced it. She also passed this love of reading onto her own children. Michaelle is the second oldest of four children. In her early years, she traveled with her family due to her father's military obligation. As a young adult, Michaelle joined the Army. Her love of learning encouraged her to follow several roads, from auto parts retail clerk to a chimney sweep to valedictorian of her LVN class. She resides today in a small Texas town with her husband, two dogs, two parrots, and various farm fowl. She still enjoys reading and now writing as often as she can.

∞

Ada James doesn't exist. At least, not in our timeline. Just ask her. She'll tell you. A masterful weaver of stories that bite, Ada crafts gripping science fiction thrillers filled with time-traveling assassins, conspiracies, and murder, alongside enchanting fantasies brimming with curses, kisses, and dragons—always dragons! Her sassy heroines are unapologetically fierce, serving up badass butt kickings flavored with a dash of romance and a generous side of snark. Her stories contain a spirit of adventure, inviting readers to join her on spellbinding journeys where the impossible becomes possible, and every story promises a thrilling escape. Raised on the Texas coast, Ada found a unique blend of inspiration and solace as hurricanes became her unexpected companions. Huddled beneath her grandmother's hand-pieced quilts, she devoured thrillers and fantasy novels by flashlight as gale-force winds whipped the shingles off the roof. Now residing in Atascosa County, when not locked away in her writing cave with her best friend/ technical advisor/husband, Ada James can be found embarrassing her multitude of children and grandchildren by dancing in the middle of a country road or searching for mud puddles to splash through.

∞

Tess Monroe lives in her own little world. Where her surroundings, thoughts and ideas, are held captive in her mind, until she pens them into the pages of her novels.

∞

Caitlyn Lasater spends her days wrangling both unruly children and equally unruly vegetables in the wilds of south Texas. When not battling her overgrown garden or grading essays that definitely weren't written the night before, she can be found with her nose buried in a book or furiously mashing her keyboard for both stories and video games. Her spouse and two children have learned to recognize the glazed look in her eyes that means she's mentally drafting her next story and mostly know better than to ask what's for dinner. Caitlyn's writing is fueled by pretend coffee at the local coffee shops (she's allergic but likes the aesthetic) and the desperate need to get characters moving from her head to her paper, as she feels guilty when they're stuck in limbo. She swears she will turn in the rest of her anthology chapters as soon as she beats this last video game level.

www.fairytalebookstore.com[1]
EMail: info@fairytalebookstore.com
Facebook: www.facebook.com/fairytalebooksllc[2]
Tel: 830-770-0049

---

1. http://www.fairytalebookstore.com

2. http://www.facebook.com/fairytalebooksllc